REAL LIFE

REAL LIFE

Cynthia Harrod-Eagles

Chivers Press • Thorndike Press
Bath, England Thorndike, Maine USA

This Large Print edition is published by Chivers Press, England, and by Thorndike Press, USA.

Published in 2000 in the U.K. by arrangement with Severn House Publishers Ltd.

Published in 1999 in the U.S. by arrangement with Chivers Press Ltd.

U.K. Hardcover ISBN 0–7540–3917–X (Chivers Large Print)
U.K. Softcover ISBN 0–7540–3918–8 (Camden Large Print)
U.S. Softcover ISBN 0–7862–2171–2 (General Series Edition)

The text of this Large Print edition is unabridged.
Other aspects of the book may vary from the original edition.

Set in 16 pt. New Times Roman.

Printed in Great Britain on acid-free paper.

British Library Cataloguing in Publication Data available

Library of Congress Cataloging-in-Publication Data

Harrod–Eagles, Cynthia.
    Real life / Cynthia Harrod–Eagles.
        p.   cm.
    ISBN 0–7862–2171–2 (lg. print : sc : alk. paper)
    1. England—Social life and customs—20th century—Fiction.
    2. Psychological fiction, English.   3. Large type books. I. Title.
    [PR6058.A6945R4   1999]
    823'.914—dc21   99–38789

'Behind the corpse in the reservoir, behind the
    ghost on the links,
Behind the lady who dances, and the man who
    madly drinks,
Under the look of fatigue, the attack of
    migraine and the sigh
There is always another story, there is more
    than meets the eye.'
                    Autumn Song VIII W.H. Auden

CONTENTS

Gardener's Question 3

Real Life 47

Vacant Possession 69

Wolf's Clothing 85

Little Devils 101

Lonely in a Stranger's House 121

Suitable 131

Loving Memory 143

First Floor Front 161

The Cakes of Wrath 191

Missing 211

Helping Hands 233

Culture Vulture 257

GARDENER'S QUESTION

GARDENER'S QUESTION

I thought at first that it was a sycamore seedling, because there was a mature sycamore two gardens down, and you know how they like to colonise the entire world, given half a chance. In early spring when I do the first of my serious weekends of gardening I pull up dozens of hopeful little trees, and miss as many more, well-hidden behind established shrubs, or in that fertile no-plant's-land between the compost heap and the fence. Eventually, however, they give themselves away, and I haul up an eight- or eighteen-incher topped with two or three handsome broad leaves. Sue, who has an absurdly soft heart, cries out in protest. She kept one on the patio in a pot for two years once, until some blight got its roots and killed it. But I think familiarity has accustomed her by now to their demise, because she no longer seriously expects me to preserve a sycamore forest in my sixty-by-thirty foot urban plot.

Anyway, this particular specimen, being well-placed behind the philadelphus, managed somehow to escape detection until it reached the top of the fence. I was balancing in the border, my feet carefully positioned in the only two empty spaces amongst the azaleas, pruning back the dead wood on the perennial fuchsia. That done, I thought that while I was in position, I might as well cut out a stem or two from the philadelphus, which was growing rather straggly, and as I stretched out my hand to rest it on the top of the fence for balance, I found myself looking at a strong horizontal branch I didn't recognise.

Frowning, I traced it back until I came to the trunk, and thus bit by bit worked out the outline of the whole tree. It was extraordinarily difficult to see and it took me a while to realise that it was because the colour of the wood seemed to tone in perfectly with whatever it was resting against. Camouflage is common amongst insects, and not unknown in the plant world, but I have never seen this kind of chameleon ability to change colour in any other vegetable growth.

As well as this unnatural capacity, the tree had an indefinably alien look to it: somehow it didn't seem to belong in the garden of a semi in Ealing. At that time, when I first saw it, it was about six feet high, a perfect little tree in miniature. Its trunk I could just span with my two hands—about six or seven inches in diameter, I suppose—and all along the branches were leaf-buds, elongated and silvery-olive in colour.

'Sue!' I shouted. 'Come and have a look at this!'

She came, and stared for a long time before she could really pick out the shape of it. 'What is it?' she asked.

'I haven't a clue. It must be self-seeded.'

A cloud swept across the sun at that moment, and as the shadow crossed the tree's trunk, we both saw clearly for the first time the curious fluctuation of its colour as it matched the fence behind it.

'How very odd,' Sue said mildly. 'What kind of a plant does that?'

'It isn't anything I recognise,' I said. 'We must get out the big gardening book after lunch and have a look at the tree section, see if we can spot anything like it.'

'It looks,' Sue said cautiously, 'sort of foreign, doesn't it?'

'I know what you mean. But there are so many exotic plants and fruits coming into the country nowadays that there's no knowing what you might find.'

'Do you think it's a fruit tree? I suppose some bird might have dropped the seed as it flew over. It's got a sort of Mediterranean look about it, hasn't it?'

I smiled at her affectionately. Women say such daffy things sometimes. 'Mediterranean? Darling!'

'You know, sort of hot sunshine and cicadas,' she insisted. 'Sort of Biblical.'

'Biblical is Middle East, not Mediterranean,' I pointed out.

'Whatever,' she said. 'But if it is from a hot place, it probably won't grow true to its nature

5

in our climate and soil.'

'You mean we're harbouring a freak?' I said in mock horror.

'But you won't pull it up, Mike, will you?' Sue said anxiously.

'It's past pulling up,' I said. 'It's too big for that. I'd have to cut it down.' I laid a hand thoughtfully on the trunk, and—I know it sounds silly—but I swear it trembled. I felt it quiver under my touch, and at the same moment the slender outer ends of the branches moved quite rapidly, though the wind was still at that moment. I snatched my hand away.

'Oh, please,' Sue said, 'let's keep it a while. I'd like to see how it turns out. And it's done so well so far. It would be mean to kill it when it's tried so hard.'

I gauged the distance between it and the fence. 'In a couple of years at the most it'll be pushing the fence over,' I said, but Sue smiled, knowing from my voice that she had won.

'Thanks,' she said.

'You're the only person I know who literally wouldn't hurt a fly,' I said affectionately. She wouldn't, you know. She'd feed the greenfly, given a chance. 'Give me a hand out, will you?'

'I think it's going to be rather pretty,' she said as we stood together on the path looking at her new protégé. 'If it is a fruit tree, there'll be blossom, won't there?'

6

*　　　*　　　*

Sue was right—it did turn out to be a pretty tree. We saw its leaves for the first time that year, and they were a longish oval in shape, very dark green and shiny like a camellia's, but silver on the underside, so that when they moved in the wind, the whole tree seemed to shimmer and flicker with light. As soon as it was reprieved, it seemed to shoot up, as if it had gained confidence, and by the end of the year it was nine or ten feet tall.

Meanwhile I looked through all my gardening books, but I couldn't find anything that more than remotely resembled our tree. It didn't much surprise me, however. As I'd said to Sue, there were all sorts of strange things being brought into the country, by migrating birds, aeroplane slipstreams and returning holidaymakers. You only had to go and look at a landfill site or a piece of waste ground to see the colonising exotica that flourished there. I did think about going to the library and doing a bit of research, or phoning up *Gardener's Question Time*, but you know how it is—life's too short. Anyway, it didn't seem important. To tell the truth, I'm not a dedicated green-finger merchant. Sue's the keen one. Apart from my two weekends a year and the weekly trot round with the mower, my gardening consists of sitting out on the patio with a tall glass of something that clinks. So after the first

7

couple of weeks, I forgot all about the tree.

It was towards the end of summer that Sue drew my attention to it again. She works from home, so I suppose she has more time to notice things than I do.

'You know,' she said thoughtfully one day, as we sat side by side on sun-loungers, enjoying a drink while the supper cooked, 'you know, there is something odd about that tree.'

'What tree?' I asked absently. I was contemplating, with an anticipation I couldn't really share with Sue, the trip to Frankfurt which was coming up in a couple of weeks. Trade fair. Bound to be a bit of a jamboree. The clients always let their hair down at these things, and we came in for a lot of the crumbs from their tables.

'*The* tree,' Sue said, with a touch of impatience.

'Oh, that tree,' I said, with a lack of interest that would have alerted a less single-minded woman to the fact that my glass was empty.

'I can see it from the window of my room,' she said. 'I watch it quite a bit, and it's definitely odd.'

'Odd how?' I said indulgently, and she gave me a frown, as she does when I don't take one of her projects seriously.

'Well, for one thing, it's very hard to see.'

'I thought you said—'

'Yes, I know what I said. What I mean is, even when you're looking straight at it, it just

8

seems to—I don't know—fade into the background.'

'Natural camouflage,' I said. I remembered that I had noticed something like that myself that first day. 'There are moths like that, that look exactly like tree-bark. Do you remember—'

'No, I don't mean that,' she said. 'I mean that when you look at it, you can see it all right for a moment, and then you just—sort of—can't.'

'Oh darling, don't be silly.'

She gave me a flashing blue glance, like a cross Siamese. 'You try it,' she said, 'and see if I'm not right. It seems to know when you're looking at it. If you glance at it sideways you can see it, but when you look straight at it, it disappears. Go and try it.'

'If you say so,' I said placatingly. I wasn't going to get up and walk all the way down the garden to look at a bloody tree, when I'd just got comfortable. 'It's the same with animals in the undergrowth, isn't it. I mean, deer and zebras and things,' I added vaguely.

She was hardly listening to me. 'And another thing,' she said, 'it moves when there isn't any breeze.'

I stirred myself to look at her. She was quite serious, even a little anxious. 'You're not going to get a triffid complex about this thing, are you, darling, just because we don't know what it is? It's just a perfectly ordinary tree, species unknown.'

'I have not got a complex,' she said sharply. 'It moves.'

'All right, it moves,' I said placatingly.

'And don't patronise me. I know what I've seen. It moves as if it's feeling a breeze from somewhere else. As if it's got its roots in our garden and its head somewhere else entirely.'

I hoped she wasn't going to start going fey on me. Usually she was as level-headed as the next person—but of course, women can be odd at certain times of the month, and you just have to ride it out. 'But look here,' I said reasonably, 'the leaves on a tree are never really still. They move about in the tiniest air movement, even when you think it's a perfectly still day. Just take a look at the other trees, and try to keep a sense of proportion.' She didn't answer, but the look she gave me was eloquent. 'Look, if it really bothers you, I'll cut it down, and that'll be the end of it.' It was a brave offer, as you'll know if you've ever tried cutting down a tree—to say nothing of digging out the stump afterwards—but I was relying on her tender heart to bail me out.

It didn't fail. 'Oh no,' she said quickly, 'we mustn't hurt it.'

'Softy!' I said, relieved. Although afterwards it seemed to me that what she had said was a little odd, I didn't know why. Perhaps it was the tone of her voice—she had sounded almost afraid.

10

After that the Tree disappeared from our conversation and I forgot about it again; until the day came when I was forced to face up to it that my putting-the-garden-to-bed weekend couldn't be postponed any longer. So it was on with the cords and wellies, and out with the fork and the secateurs.

'It's a nice, still day, at least,' I said, 'so we can have a bonfire for the leaves and rubbish without all that aggressive window-banging we had last year from Mrs Thing over the back.'

'She had just put her washing out,' Sue mentioned.

'She didn't put it out until she saw us building the bonfire, the old bag. Anyway, she shouldn't do washing on a Sunday.'

'Traditionalist,' said Sue, and threw a trowel at me. It hurt. She keeps herself fit, does Sue. Goes to the gym most days—to counteract sitting in front of a computer for hours on end, she says.

The bottom of our garden was a hedgehog's paradise of dead leaves, and I got out the rake and dragged up a huge heap of them. The Tree seemed to be holding on to its leaves better than most, for which I offered up brief thanks for small mercies. In fact, most of them were still green, and didn't look like falling at all, as if the Tree was trying to be evergreen and not quite making it. I remembered what Sue had said about not growing true in our climate, and wondered if it were evergreen in

11

its own place. But anyway, the leaves that were turning were gold on the top and silver underneath—rather attractive. Like a money-tree, I thought. I leaned on my rake for a breather and contemplated it, and then a strange thing happened.

As I said, it was one of those still, hazy days you get in autumn, the sky a sort of misty blue, the air warm and motionless; but suddenly the leaves of the Tree were rustling, and the thinner branches were bending back and forth quite strongly, as if in a moderate, fitful breeze. I looked around at the other trees nearby. The apple tree, only feet away, was quite still, its remaining leaves hanging motionless. I looked back at the Tree, and saw all its branches bend suddenly one way, as if in a strengthening of breeze that wasn't happening anywhere else in the garden.

I tell you, it was very queer. I dropped the rake and moved closer to it, though I was beginning to have an uncomfortable feeling about it. The leaves were making a rustling sound, and as I got nearer it began to sound like human voices, like a large crowd of people all whispering together.

Triffid complex, I told myself with an attempt at firmness; but I watched, fascinated, as a dying leaf detachcd itself and whirled horizontally for a few feet, before almost literally stopping in mid air, and then drifting slowly down to earth in the most natural way.

For once, the Tree was perfectly plain to see, and as I inched another step forward I found myself thinking that it hadn't noticed me because its mind was on other things. Absolutely daft! But it had the air of enjoying itself in that refreshing breeze, busy swaying and whispering to itself, so that it had no attention to spare for hiding from me. Despite the swaying, I felt no movement of air on my own face. It was as if the Tree was growing in another world.

One last step, and I was close enough to look through the branches of the Tree into next door's garden. Now this is going to sound loony, but it really happened—or at least, I think it really did. I mean, I remember it very clearly, so what does that mean? Anyway, what happened was this: I looked through the branches, and instead of next door's rather neglected suburban plot, I saw a completely different garden, crowded with trees and shrubs, undergrowth and creepers, and short, dark turf in between. It was so green and lush it seemed to be bursting with life—you could almost hear things growing—and just for a second a delicious, wet, green, verdant smell came to me on the breeze, and I could see by the sharpness of the shadows that the sun was very bright and high overhead. No wonder the Tree was excited, I thought. The whole place was pulsing with plant life. And the thought came to me that I was seeing the Tree's own

13

place, where it came from and where, for half the time, it still lived.

All that takes time to write, but it took no time at all to see and smell and feel. It lasted only a second, but it was so vivid and real that I remember it still as clearly as if I had stood gazing at it for hours. And even now, the memory fills me with a kind of aching feeling of loss.

But the next instant the vision, or whatever it was, had vanished. I was looking at next door's lawn and scrawny roses again, and the Tree was perfectly still, its leaves hanging motionless. Everything was normal.

I was shaken, I can tell you. I'm not religious and I've never been into all that supernatural stuff, other worlds, ghosts, horoscopes and all that guff. But I can't help it, I saw what I saw. Afterwards I had to go and sit down for a bit, until Sue, thinking I was slacking, came and rousted me out. Then human adaptability got to work, and I pushed the experience away into the mental oubliette one keeps for the inexplicable, and forgot about it. I didn't say anything to Sue about it. One doesn't want one's own wife giving one funny looks and edging towards the door. Besides, the next week I was off to Frankfurt, where I met Jenny, an off-duty BA stewardess, who completely bowled me over. She had blue-black hair and a sensational body, and was completely bowled over by me, too. From

14

then on I had plenty to occupy my mind—and plenty, also, to conceal from my wife.

During the winter the old lady who lived next door died, and the house was put up for sale. Various people came to look round, and we kept our fingers crossed, because neighbours can be heaven or hell. It mattered more to Sue than to me, of course, since she was at home all the time. Since the advent of Jenny, I was hardly there at all those days. Finally the sold notice went up, and a couple about our age appeared with tape measures and nodded to us over the fence.

He was tall and sandy-haired, with a small, neat moustache and an educated accent. He wore cords and an Arran sweater and I took him to be a teacher or something in the social services. She was tiny with straight red hair and frightened brown eyes, wore a very unglamorous anorak and no make-up, and never seemed to say a word. They moved in with two small boys, and soon builders and decorators were in and out, and we stopped holding our breath and relaxed. They were going to be all right.

She turned out to be Scottish; he came from the Borders, Hadrian's Wall country: when you listened long enough you could just catch a faint lilt of something in his otherwise educated-neutral accent. Sally and Graham were their names, though we didn't have occasion to use them. As I said, I wasn't home much at that time, and the first real contact I had, beyond the polite passing nod and greeting, was in the spring, when I was out in the garden one Sunday afternoon. The teacher was out too, digging away in the border nearest our fence with a fine display of muscular athleticism. Our eyes met, and there was nothing for it but to converse.

'You've got your work cut out,' I observed. 'It's very neglected.'

He rested his foot on the top of his fork and said, 'Yes, I suppose the old lady who was here before couldn't do much. I'll soon get it sorted out, though.'

'Keen gardener?'

He smiled. He had small, very neat teeth under the small, very neat moustache. 'Fair to middling,' he said, in the modest tone that real fanatics use about their passions. 'I find it restful after coping with adolescents all day.'

I patted myself on the back for perception. 'Teacher?'

'I'm a lecturer at the poly,' he said. 'Anthropology.'

'Ah,' I said. Close enough. 'That sounds interesting.'

'Oh, it is,' he said, and seeing I was not really interested, he changed the subject. 'That's an odd sort of trcc. I'vc been wondering for some time what it is.'

I glanced at the Tree. It hadn't half grown during the winter. 'I haven't a clue,' I said. 'It

16

just appeared—self-seeded.'

He jammed his fork upright in the earth and came closer. 'I thought at first it was a medlar, but the bark isn't quite the same, and the leaves are all wrong. What's the fruit like?'

'It hasn't ever fruited.'

'Well it will this year,' he said, pointing. 'Look, see the flowers?'

'Good Lord, yes,' I said. I hadn't noticed them before. Very small, rather dim, and well-hidden.

He stuck his hands in his pockets, staring at the Tree. 'It certainly is odd,' he said. 'Have you noticed—?' But he changed his mind about whatever he was going to say. 'Interesting tree, the medlar. Supposed to be the original Tree of Knowledge—you know, the Garden of Eden tree, the Adam and Eve and Serpent thing.'

'Oh, really?'

'Yes, that's what they think now, because the medlar comes from Persia, where scholars believe the real Eden actually was, and also because the medlar's fruit is only good to eat when it's rotten.' He looked at me enquiringly to see if I understood. Him lecturer, me office-worker; me velly thick. I played up to him.

'Oh yes, I see. Very philosophical, that,' I said. 'Is that part of your subject? I've often wondered what anthropology was.'

'Biblical studies were my second subject,' he said. 'Sally and I are keen church-goers. She

17

was an RI teacher.'

'Ah,' I said, concealing my alarm. 'We don't indulge, I'm afraid. Sue's a lapsed Catholic and I'm a lapsed atheist.'

He smiled as though I'd made a joke in bad taste. 'Well, I must get on. I shall be interested to see what sort of fruit you get from that tree, though.'

'I'll keep you posted,' I said, and headed indoors for a stiffener. Funny how religious people make you nervous.

*   *   *

During that spring and summer my affair with Jenny took up more and more of my time and mental energy. What had begun as merely good fun took on a more serious edge. We could not get enough of each other, and because of her working schedules and my marital situation there were many frustrating occasions when we could not be together. It made us both edgy and miserable; added to which I had bad guilt feelings about Sue. We had been married nine years and I was still very fond of her. We had always got on well together and the house was comfortable, and frankly, the thought of leaving her and going through all the hell of a divorce didn't appeal in the least. But in the back of my mind I suppose the thought was growing that some time or other the problem would have to be

18

faced up to and dealt with, because it was obviously what Jenny wanted, and she was beginning to drop hints that it was getting more and more difficult to ignore. For my part, I just wanted to put it off as long as possible. I suppose like everyone else I would sooner have my cake and eat it, if I could possibly manage it.

In July I managed to have four glorious days with Jenny by pretending to Sue that I had to go away on business and telling them at work my father had died. That's the sort of excuse you can't repeat too often, of course. But then, about a fortnight after I got back, Sue played into my hands by telling me that she wanted to go off on a holiday on her own.

'On your own? Where to?'

'Somewhere remote and empty. Like Northumberland, for instance,' she said. 'I just want to get away by myself. You've had your trip—I know it was business, but I've been cooped up in this house for months, and I need to get away, just for a bit. Blow the cobwebs away.'

She looked at me a bit apprehensively, as though she thought I was going to come the Heavy Husband; but it was all I could do to act as if I would miss her.

'You don't need to justify yourself to me, darling. You go. You deserve a break. Stay as long as you like.'

So she went. She was away a week, and I

hoped she would have a good time, I really did. I was feeling half despicable, half blissed-out, because I phoned in sick and spent virtually the whole time in bed with Jenny.

One odd thing happened during that week. I didn't think much about it at the time, but it became odder with retrospect. Jenny was at our house that day (I knew it was safe because Sue had phoned me from Northumberland that morning so I knew she couldn't walk in on us) and I wanted to show her some photographs of an old campaign I had been involved in which had pretty much become a classic. They were in a cardboard box in the loft, but when I went to look for them I couldn't find the key that worked the loft-ladder. After a fruitless search I gave up and went downstairs. Jenny had wandered out into the garden. I found her standing gazing dreamily up into the Tree. It had grown so much that its branches now reached right out over the bed. Standing on the lawn you could almost reach up and touch it.

'No good,' I said. 'I can't get into the loft. Sue's put the key-thingy away in one of her safe places and I can't find it.'

'What key-thingy?' Jenny asked absently, without looking round. The Tree swayed in one of its private breezes, and a branch dipped down towards her.

'The key that operates the loft-ladder so that you can pull it down,' I said.

20

Jenny reached up and caught hold of the moving branch and pulled it down towards her. 'It's right at the back of the top left-hand drawer of the dressing-table,' she said.

'You what?' I asked, surprised.

She let go the branch and it sprang back up out of reach. 'What?' she said, turning to look at me. She seemed startled.

'No, I asked first,' I said. 'Why did you say that, about the key?'

'Oh—it—it seemed like the sort of place someone might put it,' she said unconvincingly. I looked at her a bit strangely, and she blushed and turned away.

I went upstairs and looked. The key was there all right. It all seemed a bit queer to me, and stalling for time, I went up into the loft and got the box of stills out, taking my time about it. When I came down, Jenny was still out in the garden. I mixed a couple of gin-and-tonics and took them out—with the photos— to the patio, and Jenny joined me.

'The key was there all right,' I said. 'How did you know?'

'Lucky guess,' she said, with a light laugh. 'It's where I'd put it. Call it woman's intuition.'

I let it pass. It didn't seem important. We sipped our drinks and looked at the stills, which she admired enormously. I think until then she hadn't realised that what I do is an art-form as well as a commercial necessity. In the next-door garden the neighbour's kids were punting a football back and forth—quite a peaceful, Sunday sort of sound. Suddenly Jenny said, 'Your neighbour's boys, are they called Jason and Toby?'

'I'm afraid so,' I said—rather wittily, I thought. I supposed she must have heard them calling to each other.

'And did Toby cut his knee very badly at school last week and have to have stitches?' she went on.

'Good Lord, I don't know. I don't have anything to do with them, though Sue chats with Mr over the fence now and then. Why, do you know them?'

'No,' she said. 'No, not really.'

'What d'you mean, not really?'

'Oh, I mean not at all. I've never met them. It's nothing—forget it, please.'

She changed the subject firmly and I thought nothing more about it. It was only much later that I wondered . . .

At the end of the week Sue came back, looking brown and rested—thinner, too—and said she'd enjoyed her break. She seemed the better for it, but it soon wore off, and she went very quiet—not altogether happy—too quiet, spending long hours in her work-room or else brooding at the bottom of the garden, as if she was trying to avoid me. I did wonder with a brief spasm of panic whether she could have found out about Jenny, but I dismissed the idea. It wasn't Sue's way: if she had found out she'd have broached it with me. She was always up-front about everything.

A week or so later, I was out in the garden, and Graham came out into his. We caught each other's eye over the fence, and I nodded civilly. He nodded and looked away, hesitated, and then came over towards me. He seemed not entirely at ease, as if he was about to get something over with that he wasn't looking forward to. I wondered for a delirious moment if he had seen Jenny and me together and was going to say something, as a good Christian. But of course he didn't. In fact, when I came to think about it, I hadn't seen him around for a while. I wondered if he'd been away.

'I see your tree is getting its fruit at last,' he said, friendly enough.

'Oh, is it? I hadn't noticed. I'm not the world's most dedicated gardener, you know.'

'Well, I think it's probably got more fruit on our side than yours,' he said, 'this side being south-facing.'

I looked more closely and, with a bit of squinting and moving my head about, I spotted them all right: small, round, green-turning-brown things. Very dull. 'Oh yes,' I said.

'Quite a few have fallen on the grass on our side,' he said. 'They do look rather like medlars. Have you ever tried eating one?'

'Not likely!' I laughed. 'I don't put anything in my mouth you can't buy at Tesco's. You're welcome to try them if you like.'

23

He didn't laugh. 'No, I think you're wise. I always tell the children not to eat strange berries and so on. But I thought I might take one into our botany department and see if they can throw any light on it.'

'Be my guest,' I said. He nodded and was turning away when I said, 'How's Toby's knee? Stitches out yet?'

'Yes, it's all healed up, thank you.' He looked at me. 'How—?'

'Oh, I heard them talking over the fence,' I said vaguely, and left it at that. I don't know what random impulse had made me ask, but I certainly didn't expect it to have any repercussions. I found out how wrong I was a couple of days later.

That day I actually got home early for once, and thought I would earn myself some Brownie points with Sue, but as I pulled up I saw her car wasn't there. She must be out. As I got out of the car I saw next door's curtains twitch, and a face appear and hurriedly disappear again. I headed up the front path and had just got the key in the door when Graham came out and said, 'Excuse me,' in a loud, tight voice. I turned. His face was rather red and very grim, and he had the light of battle in his eye. 'I'd like a word with you, if you don't mind,' he said. In the doorway behind him Sally appeared, mouselike, and seemed to be protesting about something and plucking feebly at his sleeve. He shook her off angrily, never removing his glare from my face. 'In private.'

Oh, bloody hell, what now? I thought. My guilt circuit produced Jenny again, naturally, but I really couldn't believe even Mr Committed Churchgoer would think that was any of his business.

'What's it about?' I said coolly. 'I'm rather busy. Can't it wait?'

'No, I think not,' Graham said. 'I want to talk to you, and I want to talk to you now.' There was only a low iron railing between his front path and mine, and he stepped over it, onto my territory. I felt myself bristle and wanted to slug him one (which faintly surprised me, as I have never thought of myself as the animal, physical sort: me for sophistication and urbanity every time) but I noted at the same time that, close up, he was taller than me, and though not heavily built was a wiry sort of individual. He was certainly angry about something, and if there was any slugging to be done, that would give him the edge.

'Oh all right,' I said with a show of ungraciousness. 'But make it quick, will you? I've got a lot of work to get through tonight.'

He practically bundled me through my own front door, closing it behind me, and, feeling threatened, trapped in the confines of the hall with him, I stepped into the living room where I could put a bit of space between us. 'Well,

25

what is it?' I asked loftily.

He was seething. 'You are lucky I haven't gone straight to the police,' he said in a low voice that quivered with the effort of restraint. 'If I was a hundred percent sure, I would have. As it is—I want to hear your side of it first.'

'My side of what?' I said, surprised and dismayed by the sudden introduction of the police. 'What's all this about?'

'It's about my son Toby,' he said through gritted teeth, 'In whom you've been displaying such a particular interest.'

'Oh, good God,' I said, disgusted. I mean, okay, child abuse is beyond the pale, but these days everyone's gone paranoid about it. You can't so much as smile at a baby in a pram or push a kid out of your way in the street without being accused of trying to fondle the little bastard. 'All I did was ask you if his knee was better,' I said. 'If you're going to try and make something of that, well, it's just pathetic—'

'You know very well what I'm talking about,' he snarled. 'I know your type. It's bad enough that there are people who can't keep their hands off little boys, but your sort is even worse. You haven't even got the guts to be out in the open about it, you have to work in the dark, sneaking around whispering and insinuating, pouring poison into young minds—'

'Oy!' I shouted, desperate to interrupt him.

26

'What in the name of God are you talking about? And who the hell are you calling a pervert?'

'Don't you dare bring God's name into this!'

'I'll bring anybody's name in I feel like! Now if you've got something specific to accuse me of, let's hear it; otherwise, get out of here before I ring my solicitor. I'm not standing here in my own house being slandered with innuendoes.'

His eyes widened and I did think for a moment he was going to lash out, but he drew a deep shuddering breath and got control of himself, and said in a quieter voice, 'You want me to be specific? All right. My little boy Toby, who is only five years old, has suddenly acquired a full and detailed knowledge of the facts of life, which Sally and I decided he wasn't old enough for yet by a long chalk.'

'Now, wait a minute—'

'And not only the facts of life,' he went on, overriding me like a steamroller, 'but a whole lot of other facts that I would never want a child of mine to know—disgusting things— perverted, to use your own word.'

'My God, you have the coolest bloody cheek I have ever come across,' I interrupted him in sheer amazement. 'Do you really have the unmitigated bloody gall to suggest that I—'

'He told us!' Graham snarled. 'You can save your breath denying it. You've been talking dirty to him—to my son—to that innocent little boy—'

'*You* are crazy,' I said. 'Seriously off your trolley.'

'Pouring your insidious poison into his ears in the most underhand, sneaking, disgusting way—'

'Shut up!' I bellowed, and actually got through to him for a second. 'Now just get a grip on yourself. I can see you are genuinely upset, so I won't immediately break your neck or slap a writ on you. Let's see if we can get to the bottom of this. Just tell me plainly and without embroidery what this kid of yours has been saying.'

Graham was trembling with emotion, but he took a hold of himself, and I could see in his eyes that I had impressed him, that he was beginning to think he might have made a plonker of himself. 'Toby came in today,' he said in a quavery voice, 'and started telling Sally things—talking to her about things he— about—'

'The facts of life, yes, I got that bit.'

'She was shocked—appalled. We decided ages ago what we'd tell the kids and when, and neither of us had broached the subject with Toby, let alone told him things like *that*. She asked him where he'd heard all that horrible stuff and he said—he said—'

'Yes?' I prompted impatiently.

'He said he'd been playing in the garden,

over by the fence—*your* fence—and that someone had whispered it to him.'

'Whispered it?' I could hardly believe my ears.

'Someone in your garden,' Graham said, increasingly shamefaced, 'had whispered it to him from the other side of the fence.'

I shook my head, staring at him in a sort of broad pity that I thought would affect him more than indignation. I was right. 'And you just blithely assumed that I'd been entertaining myself by squatting down in my garden border and talking dirty to your kid through the fence? You must be barmy. Does it sound likely? Did it never occur to you that he might be making it up? Some older kid has obviously told him all that juicy stuff, the way kids do, and realising Mummy's up the wall about it he makes up the first cock and bull story that comes into his head.'

He was crimson now. 'That's what Sally said. But—'

'I should think she would,' I said, pretty mildly, considering.

'But after you'd asked about his knee—'

'Is that all it takes these days?'

'I'm sorry,' he said after an awkward pause. 'I seem to have made a bit of a fool of myself.'

'More than a bit,' I said.

'But—if you'd heard the stuff he came out with—'

'Look here,' I said, 'I've been out at work all

29

day. You can check with them if you don't believe me. I'm out all day every day. That ought to convince you if nothing else does.'

'Yes, I should have thought of that. I'm sorry.' He shook his head. 'I wish I knew where he got it from, though. I'd like to—'

'Most probably some other kid. You know what they're like.' Though I rather suspected he didn't.

He avoided my eye. 'You're taking this very well. I don't know why you should.'

'I could see you were really upset,' I said magnanimously. 'But if you don't mind, I am rather busy, so if you've got it all off your chest, I'd like to have my house to myself.'

'Yes, of course. I'm sorry. I'll go. I'm sorry.' He took himself off, muttering, but still, as I closed the front door behind him, he looked back at me with a look of loathing, as if he'd only convinced the top bit of his brain, and the deep, dark, jungly bits still believed I was a closet pederast.

I had to have a stiff drink to steady my nerves after that. Then I went upstairs and changed out of my work suit, had a wash, came down and mixed another, rang Jenny and got her answer-machine, damn it. Then I wandered out into the garden for a breath of air. It was an automatic action, and only when I stepped out did I think maybe the garden was going to be an embarrassing place to be from now on. But the next-doors were indoors, and

I had the place to myself. I walked down to the end, looking at this and that, and then paused by the Tree, sipping my drink and gazing at it absently.

It was quiet this evening, its branches quite still despite the little breeze that was stirring everything else in the garden. Its trunk was almost invisible against the fence, but its branches were clearly outlined against the sky, and the brown fruit, which had swelled considerably in a couple of days, no longer looked dull, but fat and ripe and rather tempting. I moved closer. The branch that reached out over the bed to the edge of the lawn seemed laden with them, and they were hanging there, just above my head, seeming to invite the touch. I wondered what they would taste like. They had a most attractive smell, fresh, fragrant, almost spicy, like the best sort of apple; and I thought surely nothing poisonous could have such a deliciously wholesome smell.

The desire to taste one came over me so strongly that I found I had automatically put out my hand to pick one. Seeing my hand there in front of my eyes made me pause and think that perhaps this wasn't a good idea: I was a town boy, brought up with a healthy suspicion of unknown berries and pretty toadstools. But the next moment the branch dipped a little and the movement placed one of the fruit actually in the curve of my palm. It

31

fitted so neatly, so perfectly, and the touch of the fruit's skin was so warm and smooth and delightful, that it was the work of instinct to close my fingers round it and tug.

There was no resistance. It must have been perfectly ripe and ready, because it came away as if it had been about to drop anyway. I lifted it to my lips. The scent of it was so delicious my mouth started watering in instant anticipation, and almost in a reflex reaction I set my teeth into it and bit.

It was the most delicious thing I have ever tasted. Even now I remember it with a pang of longing, because after it nothing I have ever eaten has tasted as good, and I know that nothing ever will. Beside it the best apple in the world is dull and dry, the most perfect pear is woolly, the most succulent peach tasteless. It has spoiled me for any other fruit. I have tasted perfection, the fruit of the gods, and never will again; and something I had not even thought about before is now lost to me for ever.

I swallowed and set my mouth against the fruit for a second bite. I was standing facing the house, and my eye was wandering absently over the façade—I wasn't thinking about anything, you understand, except the deliciousness of the fruit—when I saw something that grabbed my attention so violently it was like being smacked over the heart with an iron bar. In the window of the back bedroom, the spare bedroom, stood Sue, and she was stark naked. I could see her round breasts, the nipples staring at me like eyes, and the tuft of her pubic hair. Now, it wasn't that which shocked me so much—surprised, yes, that having got home after me she hadn't come to say hello—but after all, she was entitled to strip off if she wanted, and that window isn't overlooked except from our garden. No, what shocked me was the fact that standing beside her, also stark naked, dangly bits and all, with his arm resting over her shoulder was our neighbour, the saintly, muscular, sandy-moustached Graham.

My jaw sagged almost to my chest and my eyes must have stood out like organ stops. It wasn't just the shock of seeing them together, of realising they were having an affair behind my back, but that they were being so blatant about it. Knowing I was home—for Sue must have seen my car and Graham had seen and spoken to me—they had nipped upstairs, stripped off and done it in the spare bed, and now were displaying themselves at the spare-room window without the least concern that I might—that I almost certainly *must*—see them. The fruit dropped from my nerveless fingers and I was aware of a foul taste in my mouth, a stale aftertaste from the fruit that was sort of dry and coppery, like old blood. You know when you've had a nosebleed, and the taste of it slips down the back of your throat? Nasty!

I started running for the house. They had disappeared from the window—too late, mate, I thought, I've seen you! And in my own house, I kept thinking. That's what choked me. She betrayed me in my own house, and with a bloke like that, my own neighbour, that sanctimonious, hypocritical bastard! In my mind were images I really didn't want, of him and her, of him on top of her, of him between her legs doing things with his bloody moustache that made her writhe and giggle and groan. I panted up the garden and smashed into the kitchen with my blood boiling—only to skid to a halt with another smack-over-the-heart shock, because there was Sue standing by the sink washing something under the running tap.

And she was fully dressed. In street clothes. Right down to tights and high heels.

My jaw hinged again and my brain jibbered. Now I may not be the world's greatest logician, but I know there is no way in the world a woman could dress from scratch and get downstairs in the time it took me to run up the garden. Not possible. I've watched enough women get dressed in my life. Even dragging on a tracksuit would have taken longer than that, and tights are not a thing that can be hurried. I stood there, staring at her, my heart hammering, making 'Wha? Whu? Huh?' noises as I tried to reconcile the two impossibles in my mind.

She turned her head and looked at me. I have been a bit of a hound in my time, but I have never had a filthier look from a woman, and I hope I never will. She looked at me with black poison dribbling out of her eyes, while her hands continued to wash a large pair of scissors under the running water. Scissors? My brain was still locked and displaying 'wait' signs on its VDU, but there was something about scissors that I didn't like, that was ringing alarm bells. Some memory of a woman in the States with a silly name . . .

'Oh, there you are,' she said, much as she might have addressed a piece of chewing gum stuck to her sole which she had suddenly discovered she had been treading all over the carpets.

My 'Whu? Wha?' noises finally resolved themselves into a sentence. 'Where's Graham?' I said. Not my best effort but I was still trying to put two and two together and get something that made sense.

She didn't say 'How the hell should I know?' or 'Why are you asking me about him?' or even 'Graham who?', any of which would have been acceptable to me just then. She said, 'You bastard!'

I stood her another round of 'Whu?'

She took a step towards me, laying down the scissors (good!) and taking up the towel to dry her hands. She did these things by feel, her

35

eyes never shifting from my face. Her lips parted to show her teeth, and it wasn't really a smile or a grin, it was the way animals bare their teeth to show you what they've got in that department. To my first startled glance hers looked very sharp and pointed, like animal teeth, but then I saw it was because the edges were stained brown with something she had been eating. This was odd, but then so was everything else just at that moment.

'You bastard,' she said again. 'Here, in our own house. In our *bed*, for God's sake! You brought that slut here and did it in our bed. I could kill you for that.'

She had advanced towards me close enough so that I could see clearly the stains on her teeth and a little brown mark at each corner of her mouth of the same stuff; and I knew what it was. I could smell it—on her breath, yes, but more than that, coming from her skin, as though it was evaporating out through her pores. I smelled the spicy smell of the fruit from the Tree, but with that stale, metallic, old-blood aftertaste as well. She too had been eating the fruit. She had gone down the garden today while I was at work and had smelled it, reached up and taken it and bitten into it . . .

'I don't know what you're talking about,' I said, part of me evidently still working on automatic pilot.

'Save yourself the effort. I know all about it.' Sue reached out blindly for her handbag, which was on the kitchen table. 'All this time, all these months, all those lies. You total, utter bastard! You whoremongering swine! Well, I've put paid to your little game. I've finished it. And I've brought you a little souvenir, so that you won't be in any doubt. Here! No doubt you'll recognise it. I dare say you've run your fingers through it often enough.'

With a wonderfully theatrical gesture she plunged her hand into her bag, pulled something out and flung it down on the table in front of me. For an instant my heart contracted so violently it hurt, and when I saw what it really was it wasn't much better, because it was Jenny's hair. It wasn't attached to her scalp, which was both the good news and the bad news. The great, long ropes of silky, spectacular blue-black hair were lying there on my kitchen table, severed at the upper end by—well, now I understood the scissors. But why had she been washing them? I stared at the hair and then I looked up at Sue, and a hideous fear slowly leaked into my brain. Washing the scissors? Had I—did I— was there for an instant, glimpsed as I rushed into the kitchen, a hint of pinkness about the water swirling down the plughole in the sink?

'Oh my God, what have you done? What have you done?' I said in stark horror.

Sue bared her teeth still further, and her eyes boiled with rage. 'I've spiked your guns, that's what I've done! You won't be doing your illegal parking in that spot any more. You bastard! And to think I felt guilty! To think of all the misery I went through, thinking what a good man you were and how hard you worked and asking myself how I could do it to you. You made me feel guilty, you swine, and all the time you were up to the ears yourself!'

I heard no more. It was at that moment that bells began to ring and lightbulbs to light and I suddenly understood everything. I saw her and Graham standing at the window naked, and like one of those computer graphics I saw the scene swing round so that I was looking at it from their point of view; seeing, through the window they were standing at, the rolling Borderland countryside, the rounded green hills and grey stone walls and the bulk of the Cheviots standing up in the distance. That's why she had suddenly had that urge to go off alone—*alone*—on holiday, to Northumberland! Hadrian's Wall country! Bloody Graham's home ground!

I heard myself utter a sort of gargling howl, and the next minute I had flung myself at her with my hands flexed to grab her throat and strangle the life out of her. Fortunately, Sue is pretty strong and a lot fitter than me (all those trips to the gym—*if* that's where she was going) otherwise I might have found myself up on a murder charge; as it was she fought back with a staggering violence and we reeled about the kitchen snarling and panting and trying to

38

kill each other. I did manage to get my hands round her throat, but then she picked up the scissors and tried to jam them into my head so I had to let go her neck to grab her wrists instead. We fought until we were both too exhausted to carry on, and then, scratched and bruised and torn of clothing and hair we fell apart from each other, and she burst into tears and rushed out of the house.

When she had gone I slowly got my breath back and then began to feel a terrible, hopeless devastation come over me, a feeling of loss and misery so huge I would have liked to die right there and then just to get away from it. Reaction to all that adrenalin, of course. When I stopped trembling, I went out into the garden. I couldn't bear to stay in the house, especially not in the kitchen with Jenny's hair lying on the table like a corpse. I didn't want to think about what Sue might have done to Jenny. I felt dazed. I don't think I really knew what I was doing just then.

What I did do was to wander down the garden, towards the Tree. I was beginning to feel very sick, and a vague worry was trying to find room in my brain, that the fruit had been poisonous after all. As I walked towards it, I could see that something brown was lying on the grass under the Tree, and when I got closer I could see that it was fruit. Fallen fruit. A hell of a lot of it. Well, you talk about windfalls, but when I reached the spot I found that every single fruit had fallen off, every last one, and the ground was carpeted with them. Not only fallen, but already half rotten, squelched and split and giving off a fermenty kind of smell, as if they had been lying there a week. Whatever the Tree was, it had a hell of a short season.

The sight of all that rotting flesh reminded me forcibly that I still didn't know what had happened to Jenny. A weight settled on me. If Sue had hurt her—I didn't want to think about the unthinkable possibility—there would be a court case. Maybe Sue would go to jail. My life was in ruins, whichever way you looked at it. Groaning, I turned back towards the house. Better get it over with, find out the worst. Every muscle was aching from my mad fight with Sue; but my brain and my heart were aching even more. Nothing was ever going to be the same again.

*   *   *

Well, she hadn't killed her: Sue, I mean, hadn't killed Jenny. She'd gone there and confronted her, and then cut off her hair, that was all. Jenny had been scared as hell at the sight of those huge, sharp scissors. She tried to defend herself, but Sue had been too strong for her. Shc was only relieved that that was all she lost. 'I can grow my hair again,' she said, leaving unmentioned all the things she couldn't have regrown.

40

Jenny was terrific about it. She could have charged Sue with assault and battery, and I don't think Sue would have even defended herself, but Jenny decided against. Let sleeping dogs lie, etcetera. Sue had had some provocation, she acknowledged, and no real harm had been done. Besides, it was obviously all over between Sue and me, and Jenny was getting what she had been agitating for for months, for her and me to be out in the open, for us to live together. Everything resolved itself quite quickly. Sue packed her things and moved out and we filed for divorce. Next door's house went on the market almost immediately and, with property in those days moving so quickly, in less than five weeks they were gone. I don't know whether Sally ever knew about Graham, because of course there was no communication between mc and them after that day, but I rather suspect she did. I caught sight of her at the window now and then as I passed, and she looked as if she knew everything—I was beginning to recognise the look. Being committed Christians they had to forgive each other and stay together for the sake of the children, which I reckoned was going to be punishment enough on old Graham.

Jenny moved in with me and Sue and I got divorced. I didn't marry Jenny though—it didn't last very long between us. Somehow I couldn't view her in the same light as before.

Once she was living with me the magic was gone, the charm, the mystery. She was just another woman, with a woman's daft mind, and a woman's unpleasantly meaty smell, and a woman's irritating little ways. I couldn't even fancy her very much. I felt I knew too much about her. We fought a lot, and then she left, and I wasn't sorry.

In fact, after that fight with Sue, I found I had difficulty fancying any woman. Well, more than once, anyway. After Jenny left I'd pick them up in pubs and clubs and take them home, but after we'd done it, I couldn't wait for them to get out and leave me alone. Of course they don't like that, and there were scenes, and it all started to seem too much like hard work. I don't bother with that stuff very much any more. I just stick to the job. I've done very well in my job. I think cynicism is the major requirement for success in the advertising business.

The Tree? Well, the day after all the kerfuffle with Sue, when I'd sorted out that she wasn't going to be hauled off to jug for murder or actual bodily harm, I decided the Tree had to go. Although I hadn't suffered any ill effects from eating the fruit, I couldn't have it dropping that rotting stuff all over the border and lawn every year. Besides being nasty it would probably kill all the other plants; and it did occur to me that whoever was living next door, I could get sued if some kid ate one and got a belly-ache. And in any case, it was getting too big for a little urban garden. And it was definitely creepy. I didn't like it. I didn't want it in my garden. It would have to go.

So I armed myself with my electric chainsaw and went out to cut the damn thing down. But it turned out there was no need. I could see it was dying. It was standing there all limp and silent, the top branches already bare and withered, the rest of it brown, and a heap of dead leaves already spread below it in a carpet. The bark was coming off the trunk like great flakes of dead skin. Bits of it fell off even as I stood looking at it. I just couldn't bring myself to touch it, so I went away again. When I went out the next day, it was totally dead, nothing but bare, dry wood, which snapped and almost fell to dust when I took hold of it. It was no trouble to cut down—it practically demolished itself—and I had a huge bonfire and burned every last bit. It felt good, that bonfire. It was the best feeling I've had, I reckon, since that day of the fight with Sue.

Of course fruit equals seeds—I mean, that's what they're for, isn't it? The following spring a forest of little seedlings came up in that bed, and I was horrified and pulled them all up, practically in a frenzy, and had another bonfire just to throw them on—though they were so small they wouldn't have filled a basket. Triffid complex, I mocked myself, but then justified myself that *au contraire* it was quite rational, I

43

couldn't have another big tree growing up so close to the fence.

They kept coming up all that year, but I kept on top of them. The next spring there was another lot, though fewer than before. I had them up, too. After that it was just a question of keeping an eye on the border. There are always a few, trying to sneak up right against the fence, between the other shrubs, but they're easy enough to pull up if you catch them before they take hold. Like bad habits.

I've put the house on the market now. I'm moving to a flat in Canary Wharf—quite a snazzy penthouse, actually. I'm doing tremendously well financially, and it makes sense to live closer to work; and I haven't really got time to look after a garden. I was never a mad keen gardener anyway. There's a young couple been to see the house who seem pretty keen on it. Newly weds. Their first home. Pretty pukey the way they kept looking goo-goo eyes. Could hardly keep their hands off each other either. I wonder whether, if they take the house, I ought to warn them about pulling up the seedling trees? But what the hell—you can't nursemaid people. And the best way to learn about gardening is by trial and error, don't you think?

REAL LIFE

REAL LIFE

Commuters, thought Lessiter one evening, led lives of peculiar and esoteric misery. Oh, not main-line commuters—their plight was well understood, and their lot pitied. Newspapers studied them and had special pages devoted to them; MPs brought them up at question time in the House; there were short stories about them, and tautly-written, acerbic little half-hour television plays on BBC2.

But what of the tube commuter? Who cared for him? Main-line commuters thought themselves superior in anguish, professionals in a world where tube-train travellers were amateurs, mere dilettantes, dabbling in the thing for a frolic. Lessiter worked in an office where four of his five colleagues travelled in from Surrey and Sussex on 'real' trains, and was accustomed to the attitude. If he complained, they would only sniff, and imply somehow that it was his own fault, and served him right for not doing the thing properly and moving out to Weybridge or Reigate or Horley.

The fifth colleague was a phthisical and elderly Scotsman who lived in a bachelor flat in the Barbican, and walked into work, rain or shine. He never joined in the talk of cancellations and strikes, took his sandwiches alone, and regarded his colleagues as interesting biological specimens, of a type so little suited to their environment that evolution was bound to take care of them sooner or later.

Lessiter disliked Macpherson as one is bound to dislike those who have no need of us and are tactless enough to show it. Emotional self-sufficiency is not a lovable trait; in addition to which Macpherson seemed unforgivably immune to the common cold.

Boston Manor was Lessiter's home station. He knew it with the intimacy of tolerance and irritation, as one knows the spouse of many years, or the twelve-year-old family saloon. One end of the platform, the end where the stairs led up to the booking hall and the street, was roofed over with a scalloped Edwardian canopy. Beyond the canopy the platform stretched away under the open sky almost into the countryside. It was edged with a deep shrubbery, bleak in winter, but in spring and summer loud and quivering with birds and bees and butterflies. Sometimes Lessiter would face the shrubbery and half-close his eyes, imagining himself alone in some remote and bosky spot. The sweet tarry smell of the sleepers basking in the sunshine, and the thrilling tweet of the lines announcing the approach of a train, would come to him as true scents and murmurings of nature: for he was a town-dweller of old stock, and his soul was rooted deep in the beauty of order and the elegant converging parallels of road and railway track.

From Boston Manor Lessiter travelled daily to Holborn, a long journey, and expensive, as his colleagues so often pointed out. Of course, east London was closer to his place of work, but Lessiter was born and bred in west London, and you might as well ask a west Londoner to move east as ask a goldfish to live in a birdcage. It just couldn't be done. After Liverpool Street the very names of the stations were unfamiliar, began to sound exotic and faintly threatening, like those of Central European villages, implicit with sinister noblemen of nocturnal habit.

Going up in the morning was tiresome: delays, cancellations, strikes, the weather, and most of all his fellow-travellers. The up train came in from Heathrow, and having to share the early morning with Japanese tourists with enormous suitcases and Swedish students with backpacks was a hard thing, an undeserved burden.

Going down in the evening was in one respect worse. The Piccadilly line branched after Acton Town, and only one in two trains took the Heathrow branch on which Lessiter's station was situated. Furthermore, the station before Lessiter's was Northfields, and between Northfields and Boston Manor there was a marshalling yard. Just occasionally,

49

particularly during the rush-hour when it would annoy people most, the transport authorities would terminate a train at Northfields in order to send it to bed or turn it round. Northfields was just too far from home for Lessiter to walk from there comfortably.

It was this last undeserved brickbat of fate which gave rise to Lessiter's present bitter musings on the pains of being a tube commuter. He had arrived on the platform at Holborn just in time to see the doors of a Heathrow-bound train close, and had to wait while two useless trains passed through. When the long-promised Heathrow train rumbled in, it bore across its illuminated forehead the hateful word 'Northfields'.

Nothing burns in a man's heart more searingly than undeserved persecution. Lessiter wedged himself Pisa-like into the doorway, arched balletically out of the path of the closing doors, and seethed with futile rage, his nose inches from the armpit of a man who evidently thought deodorant effete, and considered it a frivolous waste of money to dry-clean a suit he only wore to work.

Northfields! Lessiter would have to get out at Northfields, tantalisingly just out of reach of home, and wait on a station where the winds of the Arctic and the Antarctic met and swirled eternally around each other in a mysterious ritual grit-dance.

Worse was to come: the train stopped

without explanation in a tunnel. Lessiter's outrage rose in him like milk in a hot pan when after some minutes the sound of the motor died away, leaving the passengers in a tightly-packed and speechless mass, listening to each other's breathing. It really was the last straw, Lessiter thought. His strap-hanging arm was tingling with pins and needles, and his pectoral muscles were aching, but there was no way of lowering his arm past the wedged shoulders of his nearest neighbours. He began to feel a little faint and a little sick, and told himself sternly that it was absurd to give in to claustrophobia. Besides, it simply was not physically possible to faint in his present situation.

Then he thought of Macpherson, probably at this moment sipping a glass of malt whisky in the comfort of his centrally-heated service flat, and the milk boiled over, and the carriage lights went out.

*   *   *

Lessiter thought he must have fainted after all, for he became aware of a sensation of time having passed, and of things around him being different. It was still pitch-dark, but it was also silent, and he seemed to be lying face downwards. There also seemed to be a great deal of space around him. Had his fellow passengers put him down on the floor and stood back to give him air? Another thought came to him: had they callously left him unconscious on the train, to be carried off to the marshalling yard? Surely not! Yet the silence was certainly absolute, the absence of other people as well as of the train's motor.

He tried to move, found he could not, and panicked. Something very odd had happened to him. He was lying prone—he felt his body stretching away behind him—and yet he was facing forwards. Was he perhaps on his hands and knees? He explored his sensations, and found that he was indeed supporting himself on his extremities upon something hard and narrow; but that explained nothing, for he seemed, caterpillar-like, to have more than four extremities, and they were close under his body in a way that was not possible for hands and feet to be, given his age and lack of suppleness. And besides, if his hands and feet were under him, why couldn't he move? Where was he? Where was everyone else? Lessiter sobbed aloud in fear, and then caught his breath with an even greater degree of terror at the sound he had emitted.

'What's up?' someone said, close by his right shoulder. At least, 'said' was not quite the right word. Whoever it was had communicated with him, but quite how he could not determine.

'Who's that?' Lessiter whispered, and the voice he emitted was not his, nor strictly speaking a voice at all—certainly not human.

'84410,' said the person next to him. 'Who's that?'

'My name is Lessiter,' Lessiter replied, and found the greatest difficulty in forming his name into sounds. It was quite hard to think it, too. Had he had a stroke? It seemed as though parts of his brain were not functioning as they ought.

'Name?' said the other. 'Oh, yes, I remember. You're the new one. You're 80592.'

Lessiter digested this. A number, not a name. It suggested prison to him.

'Where are we?' he asked at last.

'Northfields, of course,' said the other.

The name eased something in Lessiter. At the familiar sound of its syllables, some of his panic ebbed away. He was safe, not even far from home.

'But why is it so dark?' he asked.

The other was a long time replying, as though the question were unexpected, out of the common. 'Because it's night time,' he said at last.

'Aren't there any lights?' Lessiter asked.

'We're in the engine shed.' A completely different voice spoke from beyond 84410. In the terms in which he now judged these communications, it came from an older, more mature individual. 'The system's closed down for the night. They won't put the lights on until they come for us in the morning.'

53

The engine shed? An unwelcome and completely untenable thought was trying to edge into his consciousness. Lessiter felt the hard thing on which he was crouching, and decided it felt very much like a railway line. Cautiously he explored his sensations: his body—a long, long body—and his hands and feet—so many of them! No fingers or toes on those extremities, just—yes—flanges! He was gripping the rails with the flanges of his wheels.

'Oh my God,' Lessiter sobbed. 'It can't be true! I must be dreaming!'

'You might give the rest of us a chance to dream, and stop making that infernal racket,' said someone else on his left.

'Go easy on him, he's a new boy,' said the train on his right. 'It takes a bit of getting used to.'

Lessiter lost consciousness again.

*   *   *

A voice in his mind, booming and portentous with the distance of memory, was saying 'the souls of dead sailors go to seagulls.'

Lessiter came to himself slowly, and saw before him an open archway beyond which, shining in the pale light of morning, stretched a vista of railway tracks, crossing and recrossing and running off with the elegance of inevitability towards that single point at the end of the universe where all parallels meet at last. It was a lovely sight, he thought dreamily; and a vague pleasure warmed him at their beauty and harmony.

'Feeling better, chum?' enquired the individual next to him, upon which the full horror of his situation came home to him with cruel clarity. It couldn't be true, and yet it was: he was no longer Lessiter, he was 80592. His long silver body stretched out behind him; his numerous wheels, in pairs like a caterpillar's feet, crouched on the dead rails; he faced that lovely vista of shining rails with a glass-fronted driver's cabin whose windows were his eyes.

'The souls of dead commuters go to tube trains,' he concluded bitterly.

'Come again?' enquired 84410.

'Oh God! What have I done to deserve this?' Lessiter cried.

'Take it easy, chum. It's not so bad once you get used to it. You get to travel, see parts of London you've never seen before. Of course, there are those who don't like going underground: tunnel-shy we call them. Somehow they never get used to it, some of them. I remember we had one once, he just couldn't stand it! Couldn't get beyond Baron's Court. As soon as he saw that black hole in front of him, he just went to pieces. Mechanical failure, time after time.'

'You talking about 54565?' asked the train on his left. 'Terrible, that was. The delays he caused, you just wouldn't believe! Remember that time he got a hundred yards down the tunnel before he froze? He had us backed up all the way to Rayner's Lane. In the end they had to get one of those breakdown cabs to haul him out backwards. It was a shocking scandal!'

'He never got over the humiliation,' said 84410. 'He went completely off the rails after that.'

'You mean—?' Lessiter asked shyly.

'Derailed himself just outside Acton Town,' said 84410 briefly.

There was a respectful silence.

Lessiter broke it at last. 'Are all of you—I mean, were all of you people? Are all trains—?'

'Good Lord, no,' said the train on his left— 9265 was his number. 'Only commuters who die in transit come this way. Most of the trains are just trains.'

'How did you come to—' Lessiter hesitated to say 'die', but couldn't think of another word.

'I can't remember,' said 9265 slowly. 'It all fades, you see, bit by bit. I've been here a good, long time, and I can't remember much about the old life. This seems much more real to me. I sometimes think I've always been a train, but I know that can't be true. Only—' He trailed off into silence. 84410 spoke up more briskly from the other side.

'He's been here too long. Gone shed-happy. I remember when I first came, he told me he was a jumper. Some of the others wouldn't talk to him at first. We all hate jumpers, you see. But he isn't a bad sort really. Only he's beginning to forget everything now.'

Lessiter contemplated this new information with horror. Gradually to forget everything seemed to him an even worse fate than the one he had already suffered. 'What about you?' he asked urgently. 'How did you come to be here?'

'Fell down the emergency stairs at Russell Square,' 84410 replied with gratifying promptness. 'Running for a train. I could hear it coming in, you see. Funny,' he mused, 'how humans do that, run for trains. As if there wasn't going to be another one.'

The train beyond him piped up. 'I always wait until they're just about to make it, and then I close my doors.' A whispery, sighing noise, like steam escaping a boiler, emanated from it, which Lessiter rightly judged to be laughter. 'I love seeing 'em curse and jump about!'

'Vulgarian,' said 9265 shortly. 'Pay no attention.'

'I wouldn't do a thing like that,' Lessiter said. 'I should remember how it felt when it happened to me.'

'Not for long you won't,' 84410 said. 'When you've been here as long as me, you'll only just remember how you got here. And when you've been here as long as old 9265, you won't remember anything.'

'I will,' Lessiter protested, and then, making a firm and solemn vow, 'I shall. I won't forget. I shall remember everything.' For how else was one to make sense of it all?

*   *   *

Later that first day an engineer came for him. 'Going out your first day? Controller's pet!' said 84410, but not unkindly.

Lessiter felt a mixture of excited anticipation and deep apprehension as the man climbed into his cab. It was a curious kind of violation, half enjoyable, half frightening, culminating in the moment when the man inserted the driver's handle into his slot, and Lessiter felt himself possessed, in the control of this creature, and yet himself powerful, more powerful than any human being could ever be.

He felt for the first time the thrilling tingle of electricity as the power went on, coursing through the rails. He tasted it with his wheels and conductors, the faint sweetness of the low voltage charge on the silver lines; the strong, salty, ozone taste of the heavy voltage in the main power rail. He absorbed its strength, pulled restively against the brakes, longing to be off down that shining track towards the distant horizon, to gallop under the morning sun for that perspective point which receded for ever, promising who knew what overwhelming delights if only it could be reached?

The brakes were released, and he surged forward eagerly, realised the joy of speed and of his own amazing power, the freedom of the rails, the passage of air, cool and exhilarating, past his windows. Why, this was the life! he thought exultantly. Why had he never realised before? This was real life; the rest was but a shadow of a dream.

*   *   *

As the days passed, he learned. He was a success as a train. He had no fear of the tunnels; indeed he rather relished them, and found the first moment of rushing headlong into the mysterious black hole exciting. He learned from his drivers when he could go fast and when he must slow down for points or a sharper-than-usual curve. He learned how to brake evenly so as not to throw the passengers about, how to judge his deceleration so as to position himself alongside a platform.

He liked his work. He even liked the passengers; and remembering what it was like to be a commuter, he was kind to them, never shutting his doors on them, or sulking in rush hour when his carriages were over-full. He felt a thrill of curiously humble pride the first time he heard one driver tell another at a change-over that he was 'a good loco'. It seemed to him a fine reputation to acquire, and he worked at it, always starting without fuss, even on cold mornings, taking the points neatly, never sticking his doors or faking power failures, as some trains did in protest, or out of boredom or even spite.

As the days passed, he knew himself happy, and despite his initial determination, he began to forget things about his old life. It was easily done, for there was not always conversation in the engine shed at night. Sometimes he was positioned alongside locos he didn't know, or who had no desire to converse; sometimes, worse still, beside those who had forgotten how to. When there was talk, it was usually a discussion of the day's experiences or grumbling complaints about the weather or rush hour or the unfairness of diagrams.

Only to 84410 was he able to talk about his past life, and even then he was aware that the other loco listened out of politeness, not because he was interested. Then the day came when he could not remember what his name had been. He recalled it after considerable concentration, but it frightened him all the same.

*　　*　　*

The only thing about his new life he didn't like was the moment of drawing into a station during the peak hours, when the platform was solid with travellers. That line of bodies all along the platform edge, the row of white faces turned towards him, the seething mass of humanity backed up behind it, filled him with apprehension. He could never be sure until he was safely in position alongside the platform that someone would not stumble and fall onto the lines—or worse still, jump. All the trains, and the drivers too, feared jumpers. The drivers were given automatic sick-leave and counselling if someone jumped in front of their train. What happened to the locos, Lessiter didn't know.

It was on a winter's day, the first really cold day of the season, when a number of locos were sticking at the points in the hope of being sent back to the shed and sleeping out the day in comfort, that he saw the woman. He was coming in to Boston Manor, eastbound, at the beginning of the rush hour. He was going up to Hyde Park Corner where he would be turned to get him back to Heathrow in time to make the run up again at the peak of the heavy traffic.

She was standing out in the sleety drizzle, which was what drew his attention to her, for everyone else was huddled under the canopy at the exit end of the platform. 80592—for so he had come to think of himself of late—snorted at the sight of her, thinking her foolish to be so desperate for a seat she would stand out in the rain to keep her distance from the rest. And then she turned her head at the sound of his approach, and looked at him.

80592 felt a shock of recognition, the more strange because he did not know why he recognised her. He only knew that he felt a dim but compelling tug towards her, and he began automatically to slow down. She was at the approach end of the platform, and once he had passed her he would not be able to see her.

She seemed to be looking at him, not in the way commuters usually looked at trains, but with some extra significance, as if she knew what he was. Who was she? Why did his consciousness pull at him like a dog straining at the end of a leash? She was a small, dumpy woman in a headscarf, ankle-boots, a long black coat and large sheepskin mittens. A middle-aged woman, plain and unglamorous. She was not the sort of female that male humans whistled at, or even noticed. In her black coat, she looked like an old-fashioned widow; her face was pale with sadness, her eyes shadowed.

Then a terror washed over him, with the absolute certainty that she was going to jump. The strange tug he had felt was one of foreknowledge, that their fates were bound up in each other, that he was to be her death. She had come here, heavy with suffering, to seek him out, to fling herself into one last searing embrace that would bring her relief and darkness and peace. And there was nothing, nothing he could do about it.

Slowly he approached. Her dark eyes were fixed on him, and she moved forward towards the edge of the platform, and their progress seemed horribly and inevitably co-ordinated as though they were being drawn together by an invisible string. He tried to stop, but his driver was urging him on, using the accelerator against his braking. He wanted to cry out to her to stop, but trains have no voice that humans can understand, and his long scream of protest sounded only like a squealing of brakes.

He struggled and broke free of restraint, and was past her, galloping along the track beside the platform, with a blur of surprised white faces turning as he passed. He felt weak with gratitude, accelerating in his relief that there was nothing under his wheels but the grateful smooth hardness of the rails. The driver, cursing him comprehensively, applied the brakes hard.

Too hard! 80592 felt the violence of conflicting motions unbalancing him, rocking him this way and that. He was losing the track—*he was going to derail*! It was death to a train. His terror was so great it made him dizzy. He felt his consciousness begin to slide, slide, down a black slope. Failing, desperate, he struggled to keep his grip, felt the track slip away from him, and tumbled terrified into darkness.

*   *   *

Lessiter came back to consciousness gradually, opened his eyes slowly to whiteness and bright light. A ceiling, a white ceiling, and the gantry shadow of an IV drip-stand. He was lying on his back in what was unmistakably a hospital bed, and before he had had time to grasp the significance of that, a face loomed into view above him, craning into his line of vision. It was the familiar pale, lined face of the woman in the headscarf—bareheaded now.

A gentle, almost timid voice said, 'How are you feeling, dear?'

Understanding burst in his brain like a sob. It was his wife. Everything came back to him in a stunning access of memory, and he cried out and tried to sit up—sit up? A nurse on the other side of the bed restrained him, pressed his shoulder, his undeniably human shoulder, and said, 'Lie quite still, Mr Lessiter. You mustn't try to move.'

'Where am I?' Lessiter heard his own voice—rusty with disuse, but a human voice.

'In the hospital, dear. St Edward's. You were taken ill on the train, don't you remember?' said his wife anxiously.

'You had a mild heart attack, Mr Lessiter,' the nurse amplified. 'A very mild one, not too serious, as long as you take it easy. Doctor will be along to see you in a few minutes. Just lie still, and try not to worry about anything. We'll take care of you.'

Lessiter lay back on the pillows, and allowed his wife to possess herself of his hand. He felt numb with shock.

'I've been so worried,' she was saying, as though confessing something shameful. 'I thought you were going to die. When they told me over the phone what had happened, I thought that if you died, I just couldn't go on. Oh darling—'

'Now, Mary,' he said mechanically, 'Don't be silly.' His voice creaked out of him, like something only just barely human. 'I've had such a strange dream,' he went on slowly. 'It was so detailed—everything was so clear—just as if it were real—'

And there he stopped, a sense of futility filling his eyes with weak tears. It had been a dream after all, he thought, only a dream. He wouldn't even be able to tell anyone about it, for there is nothing more boring to the listener than the recounting of someone else's dream.

And now he was back in reality, back home. Lessiter stared at the ceiling while his wife stroked his hand, hearing nothing of her low, loving murmurs, feeling nothing for her or about her. His mind was elsewhere, his eyes on the ceiling following other visions. In his memory the silver lines lay sweet and shining, receding for ever into perspective, beckoning him—fading . . .

He contemplated real life as it lay ahead of him, and was filled only with an aching sense of loss.

VACANT POSSESSION

VACANT POSSESSION

You know what estate agents are. They have a particular way of describing things which is evidence either of an indelible rose-tinted optimism, or an 'O' Level in Applied Prevarication. 'Deceptively spacious' means if you think it's spacious, you will be deceived. 'Mature garden' means you need a machete and bearers to get down to the compost heap. 'Characterful' means gimcrack. 'Needs some modernisation' means there's no heating, no bath, and the kitchen is a damp, gloomy lean-to with a cracked earthenware sink and a single cold-water tap that drips.

So Mike and I were extremely sceptical when we first read the description of Rose Cottage. If it lived up to the eulogies of Messrs Hicks and Warburton, it was our ideal home, the place we had discussed endlessly and wistfully ever since we were first married. All the time the children were growing up, we daydreamed about moving to the country as soon as they left home. I was a country girl by birth, having been brought up in a village in Hampshire, while Mike was from Tunbridge Wells which, though a town, was close enough to green fields for him to remember them with affection.

We had very specific ideas of what the place

69

would have to be like: a cottage on the outskirts of as untouched a village as we could find, off the tourist track, but within easy reach of the M4 so that Mike could go into Town to work and we could both go up now and then for a play or a concert. It would have all mod cons, and yet have been tactfully converted, retaining its original charm and open fireplaces. There would be a pretty, old-fashioned garden, and an old wood nearby for walking the dog we would then be able to keep. If there was a stream running through the bottom of the garden, so much the better.

It began as a sort of game which Mike and I played when we were first married. We would lie in bed in our tiny flat, cuddling each other, and describing—half joking, half wistfully— the place we dubbed Mon Repos.

'It must have roses round the door,' I would say. 'And honeysuckle.'

'Honeysuckle is always full of earwigs,' Mike would object. 'But it ought to have lavender bushes beside the path.'

'A brick path, of course. And a sundial in the garden,' I would suggest.

'A stone one, with *tempus fugit* carved on it,' he would elaborate.

It was a sort of incantation of love and optimism, and the faith that young people have that everything will be All Right in the End.

Like all couples, we had our ups and downs.

I was pregnant when we married—though we were intending to marry anyway—and there was very little money to begin with. There was even less after Lucy was born, and I had to give up my job. Mike was just starting out, and his salary was barely enough for the three of us to live on. Things were tough for a long time. Then they got better; there was more money, and we moved into a better flat with a spare bedroom.

Marcus came along, and then Harriet less than a year later. With two babies and a toddler to take care of, I was so preoccupied with feeds and nappies, and always so tired, that I didn't notice Mike's discontent. I suppose like many a man before him, he felt neglected, pushed out of his own kingdom, taking second place where he was used to coming first. He started an affair with a woman at his office, and for a time it was touch and go. I discovered about it by accident, and didn't know whether to confront him with it or not. The subterfuge made him feel miserable and guilty, which made him bad-tempered, and the children, sensing the tension I suppose, were difficult and cried a lot.

At last Mike's promotion came through, meaning a change of location, a lot more money, and a house of our own. He left the 'other woman' behind in the move and I was glad I had said nothing. I doubt whether he ever realised I had known what was going on. The children finished teething, and I stopped being tired and irritable, and so the trouble blew over, as it often does.

Our fourth, little Danny, was born brain-damaged. He lived for two bitter-sweet, poignant years, and then he died. The tragedy drew Mike and me together, closer than we'd ever been, even in the first years of marriage. It changed the children, too, from snotty, demanding, middle-class brats into something approaching angels, sensible people you could talk to and rely on. We were a family again, and as the pain of Danny receded, we came to feel that his short life had had a beauty and a purpose after all.

After that came the prosperous years as the children grew up, mostly satisfactorily, and Mike and I grew middle-aged, not unhappily. Eventually Harriet, the last out of the nest, hopped off to University, and Mike and I were alone together again. In theory, that is: in practice, we were alone separately. His work seemed to take up increasingly more of his time, and it was so complicated now that there was little point in my trying to discuss it with him when he came home. Our lives fell into a pattern of division, into long days spent apart and short evenings spent together.

I don't mean to say I was unhappy. I always found things to do to keep me occupied, and when we were together, we enjoyed that placid, undemonstrative affection of couples who have grown through troubles together. We knew each other, were sure of each other, and had no need for continual displays of feelings.

But despite that, I did ask questions of myself. Probably it was simply having more time on my hands, but I began to wonder if the description of myself, to which I had become accustomed, was accurate. Housewife, wife and mother: was that really what I was? Was that all that I was? I was wife to a husband I saw for only a couple of hours a day—his secretary spent more time with him; mother to children grown up and gone away; housewife to a household so diminished, so unused, that an hour a day would service it.

The memory of the Mon Repos dreams of our early married life returned to me more frequently and more wistfully. We had no financial problems now, so there seemed to me no reason why Mike shouldn't take more time off if he wanted to. Why shouldn't we realise those dreams? I suggested, half-jokingly at first, that now was the time to look for the cottage in earnest. Mike only smiled and changed the subject, but as the idea took hold of me, he too began to get interested. I brought home some estate agents' specifications, and he encouraged me to go out and look at any that seemed promising.

'It'll give you something to do,' he said. 'You must have time on your hands with the children gone, and I'm going to be working late a lot for the next few months, on this Dubai project.'

'All right,' I said. 'Just for fun.'

It was fun: what woman can resist looking over someone else's home? Most of them were hopeless, of course, utterly unsuitable, others were borderline. I enjoyed telling Mike about them when he got home from work—usually very late, and often too tired to do more than listen with his eyes closed, giving a grunt now and then by way of response. He was very preoccupied, but I'd got used to that when he was working on a project. 'I shan't be human again until we've got it all tied up,' he would say, and I'd learned not to take it personally if he was inattentive, and either mentally or physically absent, or both.

The Dubai project seemed to be more than usually demanding, but I hoped that when it was finished, Mike would agree to a sort of semi-retirement, if I had found the right place by then. He encouraged me to go on looking. 'Don't bother with anything that's not quite right,' he said. 'Wait until you find the perfect place.'

'It could take a long time,' I said, and he gave a tired smile.

'Well, we're in no hurry, are we?'

I was as surprised as I was delighted when I finally found Rose Cottage. For once the estate agent's eulogies didn't do it justice.

Even the name was perfect. It was almost uncanny—as if some invisible presence had been listening and taking notes during our Mon Repos games, and had whipped up Rose Cottage by magic to fit the description.

'It's just heavenly,' I told Mike. 'It's exactly what we've always dreamed of, even down to the sundial—except that it says *tempus umbra* instead of *tempus fugit*. And the lattice-pane windows are original, and there's the most gorgeous inglenook fireplace in the sitting room.'

Mike only grunted. 'You might be a little enthusiastic,' I said gently. 'I'm talking about genuine twenty-four carat magic here!'

'Sorry,' he said. 'It's this project. There are complications, you see.' He hesitated as if he was going to add something, and then changed his mind.

'How much longer is it going to take?' I asked.

'I don't know,' he said absently. 'Not much longer.' He stared out of the window for a moment, and then seemed to give himself a shake and said, 'Look, why don't you arrange for us both to go and look at this place—say on Saturday?'

'You mean you're going to be here on Saturday?' I said in mock amazement. He hadn't been home for the last three weekends.

He ignored this. 'If it's all you say it is, there's no reason we shouldn't put a deposit on it right away.'

'Do you mean it? Oh darling!' I said, and went over to kiss him. 'Of course, you may not like it,' I said. But I was sure he would.

And he did. The agent showed us round on a lovely warm September day, when the roses were having a second blooming, and the sunshine hung still and heavy in the empty rooms. The owner had gone abroad six months ago, and had now decided to stay there, so the cottage was empty, perfect for our imaginations to work on. For once, vacant possession meant what it said.

There was a very large sitting room, a smaller dining room, and a good-sized kitchen below, and two bedrooms and a bathroom above. 'What about when the children want to visit?' I said. 'You don't think it's too small?'

'No,' said Mike. 'I think it's exactly right.'

Things moved fast after that. We found a buyer for our house, and started to pack—or at least, I did. There were frantic phone calls from the children about irreplaceable belongings which they had been content to leave in their former bedrooms for years but which they now could not live without. There were agonising decisions about what to sell and what to take with us, and then a painful two hours with a house-clearer, for the cottage would not take a quarter of the stuff that filled our four-bedroom semi. Mike was very noble about it, and insisted I keep all the things

76

which were mine rather than ours or his.

'After all,' he said, 'you're at home a lot more than I am. It's right that you should have your own things about you.' The Dubai project seemed to be dragging on and on; he was hardly ever home these days.

The purchase was unprecedentedly trouble free. Our purchasers were moving from rented accommodation, so there was no chain to worry about, and we were able to book the removal people with confidence. The cottage cost considerably less than the house we were selling, and the mortgage had been paid off two years ago, so our joint account was going to be extremely surprised.

The only hitch was that Mike announced at the last minute that he had to be away on the weekend of the move, and wouldn't be back until Monday.

'Don't worry,' I said. 'The removal men don't like to be helped anyway. I'm sure we'll manage. It's only a matter of telling them where to put things.'

'You're an angel,' he said, and kissed my cheek. Then he took me in his arms and kissed me on the lips, properly, and for quite a long time.

'Hey,' I said, when I got my breath back. 'This move is doing you good already. I can't wait for Monday night!'

I don't need to tell you what the move was like. Anyone who has ever done it will remember and shudder, and anyone who has never done it will be unable to imagine the exhaustion, anxiety, anguish, and rage that a firm of removers can generate in even a well-balanced adult. Compared with the experiences I've heard related by other sufferers, I came off lightly. By eleven o'clock on Saturday night I had taken possession of Rose Cottage, with only a few irreplaceable treasures smashed or mislaid. I had just enough strength left to make up the bed, eat some toast and Marmite, and collapse, to sleep the soundest sleep of my life.

On Sunday I put on my most disgusting pair of trousers and an old shirt, and worked like a dog all day putting things to rights: hanging curtains, arranging furniture, unpacking boxes, setting out and putting away. The cottage seemed to fold round me protectively, peacefully. Our furniture fitted into the spaces easily, and once arranged, looked as though it had always been there. Everything seemed so right that I knew we would be happy there.

At one o'clock I made myself a cheese sandwich and a cup of coffee and took them out into the garden in the sunshine. I sat on the raised dais of the sundial with my back against its column, and looked about me at the tangled roses, and the marigolds on which butterflies were feeding, and thought of the previous owner. 'Why on earth did you leave?' I addressed her in my mind. 'This place is heaven!'

I got so much done on Sunday that by Monday morning I was able to spare time for refinements like dusting and polishing, and ironing the clothes I had unpacked which had travelled badly. Then at eleven o'clock the postman came with the first letter addressed to me at Rose Cottage.

It was in a brown envelope, postmarked Birmingham, and the address was typed. It looked so innocent, how could I have known? And yet all the evidence had been there for me to see. In retrospect, I seemed to have been wilfully blind to what was going on; but only a man could choose this way of doing it and think it a kindness.

It was an apologetic sort of letter, hesitant with guilt, and full of all the inevitable clichés: *'We've been growing apart for a long time, but I suppose neither of us noticed'*. And, *'I love you, but I'm not in love with you any more. I am in love with Kate. She makes me feel young again'*.

He was still able to be practical. *'I've transferred half the money from the joint account into my personal account. I think that's fair. You have the cottage, and I'll need cash for a deposit on a house for Kate and me'*. Already it was Kate and me! He was fifty-two, and she made him feel young again. She was his secretary, twenty years his junior. Poor old man, I found myself thinking. Poor foolish old man.

He wrote: '*Try to forgive me. I never wanted to hurt you, but I can't help falling in love, can I? I've tried several times to tell you, but somehow I could never face upsetting you when you've seemed so contented. And I wanted you to have your dream cottage. I wanted you to have that, at least*'.

It had been *our* dream cottage; now it was mine, mine alone, filled with my belongings, my presence. For hours I wandered from room to room, like a ghost, unable to think, reading and re-reading the letter until the words ceased to have any meaning. Some time later, I found myself in the garden, by the sundial with its mysterious, optimistic motto: *Tempus umbra*, time is a shadow. I looked back at the house, and was suddenly aware that under the layers of hurt, anger, grief, shock, bewilderment, there was something else: something close to gladness.

All my life I had been Mike's wife, the childrens' mother, and my time and my energies and my very substance had been theirs to command. Now I was alone, but my life was my own as it had been long, long ago when I was a girl. Hope bloomed in that sunny garden, brooded in that peaceful cottage. All around me there seemed to be space, room to breathe and stretch and think, with no-one to please but myself.

It had been a mixture of appalling tactlessness and cowardice on Mike's part, to separate me from my home of twenty-five years and drop me here in a cottage in the country amongst strangers, when he had intended all along to leave me. As was customary in our marriage, he had not consulted me, but had simply arranged things to suit himself. Yet in spite of all, good had come of it. Without understanding it in the least, Mike had given me something he could not even have known I wanted, since I didn't know it myself. He had given me back vacant possession of my life.

WOLF'S CLOTHING

WOLF'S CLOTHING

The only thing I didn't like about working for Baring and Beadlow was Mr Keating.

I had been quite thrilled at the thought of going to work in an advertising agency, thinking it would be really exciting and glamorous, but when I got there I soon discovered that when you are a telephonist-receptionist, the nature of your employer's business doesn't make all that much difference. There are stuffy offices and informal offices, busy offices and quiet offices, and what matters are the people you work with and how quickly the day goes, not whether your firm makes kettles, corsets or commercials.

The office itself was in an old building off Holborn, close to Chancery Lane station, which was handy for me because I lived in Shepherd's Bush, and the Central Line station was my nearest. My last job had been in Fulham, and getting there and back by public transport was murder. In the end, I was glad to leave. Well, a thing like that is bound to colour the way you feel about the job, isn't it? That was a firm that made grommets. I never did find out what grommets were, but I can tell you I sent out invoices for thousands of the beastly things. An amazing number of people all over the world didn't seem to be able to live without them.

Anyway, when I was offered this job at Baring and Beadlow, I jumped at it. I thought it would be a smart modern office in a new building, all thick carpets and Swiss-cheese plants, and gorgeous young men in Gucci shirts willowing in and out, and famous actors who were going to star in the ads turning up at my reception desk. I imagined myself going home and telling Shelagh, my flatmate, quite casually, that I been chatting to Colin Firth or Neil Pearson that day—although, I don't know if you've noticed, but the actors who do voice-overs usually seem to be quite old people like George Cole and Michael Jayston. Still, who was I to turn my nose up at any celebrity? The nearest I'd ever got to hobnobbing with the greats was when I went down in the lift at Shepherd's Bush tube station with Dickie Davis, and even then I couldn't pluck up the nerve to speak to him, though I bet he knew I recognised him.

But I needn't have worried about whether the celebrities would be famous enough, because it didn't turn out to be a bit like that. The office was older, shabbier and, I have to say, dirtier than any place I've ever worked in. It was a tall, narrow building which must have been somebody's house once upon a time, with a couple of rooms on each floor, and steep narrow stairs in between. I understood how a

Victorian housemaid must have felt after I'd spent a day dashing up and down them, between reception on the first floor and the studio on the fourth, but I suppose what you lose on the swollen ankles you gain on the trimmer figure.

However, I don't think the house had been cleaned since the last of the housemaids left in nineteen-oh-thingummy, and most of the furniture seemed to have been bought about the same time. The heavy wooden desks were all splintered—the pairs of tights I ruined!—and everything was covered in dust and coffee stains. The ladies' loo had one of those old-fashioned mosaic stone floors, and of course it was chipped, which was terribly unhygienic. Only one of the hot-water taps ever worked, and the roller-towel seemed to be permanently jammed at the upper end so that when you pulled down a clean bit the soiled end didn't wind up but lay about in loops on the floor.

My switchboard was an old-fashioned PX10, and it had those mysterious patches of brown gunge on its two-tone grey exterior that all old telephone systems seem to develop. You can spend happy hours scraping them off with the blunt end of a nail-file, or rolling them off with heavy pressure of the forefinger, but you can never, ever find out what they're made of and it's probably just as well.

However, I didn't have much time to spend gunge-rolling, which was the really good thing about Baring and Beadlow, because I was kept busy all day long, and the days simply flew by. There were no celebs trotting into my reception area—and frankly, I'd have been ashamed to invite them, because though an effort had been made with two armchairs and a coffee table covered in sales brochures, at some point someone had had a nasty accident with a dye sample over the yellow fabric of the armchairs; and, far from glossy Swiss-cheese plants. All I had was a row of half-dead spider-plants along the windowsill, and a tradescantia which had got to the stage where it had a few green leaves gasping at the end of a lot of dried-out brown trailers.

But when the telephone wasn't ringing, and the boy from the printer's wasn't hanging over my desk saying they had to have the artwork for the Daisyfresh Deodorant half-double within the next thirty seconds or the world would end, I was sending out mail and wrapping parcels and ringing round model agencies and booking studios, and even doing the urgent typing, though it wasn't my job, but somehow you didn't argue about what was your job at Baring and Beadlow. That was one of the nicest things about it. Everyone pulled together, and even the Great White Chief wasn't above rolling his sleeves up—if they weren't already rolled up, which was rare—and making the tea when no-one else had time to do it.

And there was no snobbery, either, about me being only the receptionist. Everyone had their job to do, and everyone was important. Many was the time that someone from the studio would come down with a photograph of a woman riding a white horse bareback and clutching a bottle of shampoo and ask me if it made me feel sexy; or show me two different sorts of mood lighting for a tube of toothpaste and ask me which I preferred, as if my opinion really mattered. We were all part of the same team—that's what was so good.

The copywriters were my special favourites. They were really nice people, and as handsome and charming as I had imagined everyone would be, though scruffy wasn't the word! They were usually covered in ink and paste and tiny bits of cut-out paper. They used to come in asking for this and that, and reading things to me and showing me layouts and asking me what I thought; and they teased and flirted and generally made me feel terrific. I used to go home exhausted, but so happy I used to babble on all evening about the agency, until Shelagh said she wanted to scream.

As I said, the only fly in the ointment was Mr Keating, and that was largely because he used expressions like 'fly in the ointment'. Everything he said was a cliché, and he had this terrible facetious sense of humour that made me want to curl up. I said all the men flirted, and I didn't mind it, it was part of the fun, but when Mr Keating did it, it made my skin crawl. He was so obvious, and old-fashioned. He'd come in in the morning and say, 'Hello, Alison, light of my life!' I mean, 'light of my life', I ask you! And if I was making the tea, and offered him a cup, he'd say, 'Yes, I'd better get some blood into my alcohol stream.' That sort of thing. You get the picture.

He was always pretending that he lived a riotous life outside of working hours, but you only had to look at him to know he went straight home every evening and opened a tin. He probably drank cocoa and watched *Newsnight* when he really wanted to live it up. He always wore the same light grey suit, which smelled sweaty when he lifted his arms, with a red tie which I suppose he thought was daring, and black lace-up shoes with big, round toecaps and those patterns of little holes round the sides, d'you know what I mean? He had very thick pebble glasses, which made his eyes look tiny, and his hair had been dark and was going grey all over, which somehow made it look as though he never washed it. Well, maybe he didn't, how was I to know?

The thing was that no-one liked him, and they weren't thc sort to hide it, not the copywriters. They might have put up with him if he hadn't tried to make himself out to be a jet-setter, but they'd be sitting around on desks chatting about what they'd done over the weekend, and he'd come sidling up and try to join in. He always had to go one better, about all the women who'd made passes at him, the number of gin-and-tonics he'd drunk, how fast he'd driven home in his red Porsche, and how a police car had chased him but he'd simply accelerated away and lost it.

It was sad really, but the lads couldn't stand it. They took it out on him dreadfully, and teased him rotten.

'Tell us another one, Keaty! Why don't you come in to work in your Porsche, so we can all have a look at it?'

Because of course we all knew he came to work on the tube—he'd been seen going in and out of the station.

'Oh, there's nowhere to park it round here,' he'd say lamely, going all red in the face.

The trouble was, for some God knows what reason, I felt sorry for him. I can't explain it. As I said, he gave me the creeps, and I hated the way he talked, but when he came and made up to me, I sort of jollied him along, and put him off as kindly as I could. That meant not only did he spend more time making up to me than anyone else, but also that I got teased by the others into the bargain.

'When's the big day, Ali?' they'd say. 'Where's Keaty taking you this weekend—not boring old Monte again?'

'What's it like making out in the back seat

91

of a Porsche, Ali?'

'Have you tried out the new water-bed in Keaty's penthouse yet?'

Oh, I didn't really mind that: they didn't mean it spitefully, though they were a lot harder on poor Mr Keating, and sometimes said really quite nasty things to him. No, the tough bit was when he really did start asking me out. He took a long time to get round to it, and then he was so embarrassed and awkward he made me feel awkward too. I made a mess of turning him down—said I had to wash my hair, of all things! His clichés were catching.

But after that first time he seemed to have got his second wind, because he asked me quite often, and though I always refused him, he seemed somehow to have convinced himself that I liked him, and he talked to me as though we really had gone out together, and were friends. To stop him asking me every day—I couldn't go on making up excuses—I had told him I was doing an Open University course in Economics, and studied in the evenings. That worked quite well, except that he kept asking me questions about the course, and what I know about Economics wouldn't cover a postage stamp. I began to wish I'd said I was doing English Lit, because at least I had seen *Pride and Prejudice* on the telly, and I could have burbled on about that a bit. So one day, really just to stop him asking me boring questions, I let him take me out to lunch.

I shouldn't have, I know that, but I thought it wouldn't be so bad, because I chose the local pub, so we'd be in a crowd and very public, and there'd be a good chance we'd have to share a table so he wouldn't be able to say anything too dreadful. Unfortunately, the others chose that day to go to the Italian restaurant round the corner, and Mr Keating managed to get us a little round table in the corner all to ourselves, so small that our knees were practically touching under it.

But it actually turned out to be not too bad, because away from the office, he didn't seem to have to go on telling all those pointless lies, and we talked instead about what films we'd seen and who our favourite groups were. He asked me about my home life, and I told him about my flatmate and our cat, and my brothers and sisters, and he listened and seemed really interested, and was much nicer

Still, it was a mistake, because after that it was harder than ever to be tough with him and give him a really solid brush-off, and he hung about me saying stupid things and making me writhe. The copywriters got sillier and crueller; and eventually I was beginning to feel that, even though it was such a good job, maybe I had better think about moving on.

And then one day Mr Keating didn't come in to work. Later in the day someone said that it seemed his mother had died, and he would be off for at least a week, sorting out her belongings and so on. Then two of the copywriters came down and brought me a cup of tea and sat on my desk while I was doing up the mail and told me that apparently Mr Keating had lived with his mother all his life, which they thought was really funny.

'So much for the penthouse flat and the water-bed,' Chris said.

And Dave said, 'Ah, but there really was a woman in his life after all, wasn't there?'

I felt a bit cross at that, and I said, 'I don't think it's funny. She is dead, you know, and he must be feeling very upset.'

'Oh, you always did have a soft spot for him, didn't you?' Dave said.

And Chris said, 'Pity you couldn't have got him to bath a bit more often, Ali. A woman's influence, you know.'

Mrs Keating's funeral was fixed for the Friday, and Sally, the Chief's secretary, went round with a collection for a floral tribute. I must say that all the copywriters did put in, and enough was collected for a really good wreath, though Dave spoiled it a bit by saying it ought to be in the shape of a Porsche.

My bad moment came on Thursday night, just as I was about to switch the board over, when a call came up, and it was Mr Keating. He sounded very odd, but of course that didn't surprise me.

'Hello, Alison,' he said.

'Oh, hello,' I said, a bit embarrassed. 'How

are you?'

'Bearing up,' he replied, 'all things considered.'

'I suppose you want to speak to Mr Beadlow?' I said, because there was rather an awkward silence.

'No, actually it was you I wanted to speak to,' he said. 'The thing is, I wondered if you would do me a really big favour. I hardly like to ask you, really, but—well—I wondered if you'd come to Mother's funeral with me tomorrow?'

'Oh,' I said, and my heart went down into my slingbacks like an express lift. I had never before so deeply regretted that lunch!

'You see, I told Mother such a lot about you, and she so wanted to meet you, and now it's too late. But I thought that at least—I mean, I know she'd have liked you to be there—'

I just didn't know what to say. I was flabbergasted. 'I really don't think I could,' I said, and there was a ghastly silence, which made me go on babbling. 'I didn't really know her,' and then, 'I don't know if I could get time off work, and anyway, I hate funerals, they make me feel so awful.'

I could hardly have said sillier, more tactless things if I'd been going in for a competition. When I stopped, he just said, 'It's quite all right. I understand,' but the way he said it made me feel terrible.

'I'm sorry,' I said, 'really I am.'

'That's all right,' he said.

'I hope it all goes off okay,' I said feebly.

'Thank you,' he said.

'Well, then, I'll see you on Monday,' I said rashly.

He said, 'I don't know if I'll be in on Monday.'

'Oh, well, whenever then,' I said.

My guilt feelings didn't last long—I'm not that much of a martyr. By Friday night I'd forgotten all about the awful Mr Keating. I had a nice weekend at home, and went into work on Monday morning feeling cheerful. The first thing I heard from the group hanging around my switchboard was that Mr Keating wouldn't be in that day, or any day. He had committed suicide on Friday night, after the funeral, with his mother's sleeping pills.

Any story in an advertising agency is bound to be a nine-day wonder. We talked about nothing else all Monday, little else all Tuesday, and everything else from Wednesday onwards. I refused to feel responsible, and the notion that I ought to gradually annoyed me so much that I started thinking that Mr Keating was as much of a pain in the neck dead as alive.

It was about a month later that I received a letter from a firm of solicitors asking me to go and see them in connection with the estate of the late John Henry Keating. The office was only about five minutes away in Grey's Inn

Road, so I arranged to go in my lunch hour the following day.

I suppose you can guess what it was about. It seemed that Mr Keating had no relatives apart from his mother, and evidently no friends either. He had left everything to me, in acknowledgement of 'my kindness and sympathy'.

'Surely,' I said, hoping against hope, 'he didn't have much to leave?'

'I wouldn't say that. Mr Keating was a careful man,' the solicitor told me. 'He had investments both in equities and unit trusts, and substantial life insurance. After tax, the estate should be worth in the region of five hundred thousand pounds.' I reeled.

'It is true that he had few personal effects,' the solicitor went on. 'He and his mother lived in a very modest style—though I believe the car is worth around twenty-five thousand pounds.'

'The car?' I said, my heart sinking.

'A two-year-old Porsche, in beautiful condition,' he smiled.

I can't tell you how awful I felt.

LITTLE DEVILS

LITTLE DEVILS

'There are fairies at the bottom of the garden,' said Zoe, Chloe and Hannah.

Cathy, their mother, was stuffing envelopes. The election was only four weeks away. This time they were really going to give the incumbent a run for his money. No more Mr Safe Seat! 'Yes, darling,' she said.

'No, really, Mummy,' said Zoe.

'Really,' echoed Chloe and Hannah.

'What did you say?' said Cathy, looking up, attracted by the note of urgency in their voices.

'There are fairies at the bottom of the garden. Behind the compost heap,' said Zoe.

Cathy felt the passage of faint annoyance followed by faint anxiety. Her attention had been wrested from something important by what turned out, after all, to be just a game; and the compost heap was very close to her heart.

'You haven't been messing around with the compost heap, have you?' she asked sternly. 'Daddy's told you it mustn't be disturbed. You know it's the compost that gives us all those lovely vegetables we eat.'

'Don't like vegetables,' Hannah remarked *en passant*.

'Vegetables are yukky,' said Chloe, who had just started school.

'We like McDonalds,' said Zoe the spokesperson, translating. 'And oven chips, and pizza, and poptarts—'

'And Coca-Cola,' Chloe interrupted lustfully.

Cathy heard the litany with dismay. 'You don't,' she averred, with more hope than conviction.

Zoe considered the statement and rejected it firmly. 'We do. We have them at Maria's.' Maria was the childminder. 'And she lets us watch television,' she added persuasively.

'What do you watch?' Cathy demanded suspiciously.

'*Neighbours*,' said Zoe.

'And *Postman Pat*,' shouted Hannah, overcome at the recollection.

Cathy had never seen either programme, and wondered whether to pursue the line of enquiry. She (and Andrew, her husband) disapproved of television-watching for children. On the other hand, Maria was cheap and reliable, and really loved Zoe, Chloe and Hannah, and her house was clean, and she spoke nicely. One heard such horror stories about childminders that Cathy felt extremely lucky to have found Maria in the very next street.

Asking the children detailed questions at this stage might result in the necessity for a moral decision to stop using Maria, which would be extremely inconvenient. Besides, she still had over two hundred envelopes to address, there was a constituency meeting this evening, and Andrew wouldn't be home until nearly eight, which meant that someone had to take care of the girls until he could collect them.

Anyway, she comforted herself guiltily, they could surely counteract at home any unwanted influences from outside, and the girls were given such healthy, organically grown, low-fat, additive-free food the rest of the time that the occasional sweet or hamburger couldn't do them much harm, could it? Having thus argued away her qualms, she smiled vaguely at the children and said, 'Don't bother me now, darlings, I'm very busy. I must get these done.'

Chloe and Hannah, whose memories were short and easily diverted, turned away obediently, but Zoe was more tenacious, and tugged them back with an admonitory frown. They may have been sidetracked, but the main issue had not escaped her.

'Yes, Mummy,' she said soothingly to the top of her parent's head, 'but about the fairies?'

Cathy looked up with fractionally less patience than before.

'Darling, you must learn to distinguish between fantasy and reality. I know it's only play, but you mustn't talk about it as if it were real life. You see,' she explained kindly, 'it's a kind of telling lies. Make-believe is perfectly all right, as long as you don't pretend it's anything more than that.'

Zoe knew better than to argue further. 'Yes, Mummy,' she said obediently, 'but could we please borrow your camera?'

'What for?' asked Cathy in surprise.

'Well, we thought if we took some photographs of them, we could send them to the papers, and make lots of money. Or *Blue Peter*,' she added elliptically.

There were too many things wrong with this statement for Cathy to begin to correct, with a heap of envelopes beckoning her seductively. Better to pretend it was a kind of high-tech version of making mud pies. 'A camera's not a toy, you know,' she said.

'I know, Mummy, but we'd be very careful with it, and bring it straight back,' Zoe said earnestly.

Cathy considered. Zoe had grown very responsible of late; and the camera was only an old Instamatic which had originally cost five pounds. It was sturdily made, and had no film in it. She believed in trusting children, to a certain extent.

'All right, then,' she said, 'but only for five minutes, and be very careful. Don't drop it, and don't get it dirty, and bring it back to show me before you put it away. And don't disturb the compost heap. Daddy's just put a in layer of bone-meal.'

'Yes, Mummy,' said Zoe, Chloe and

Hannah, and rushed away excitedly.

*   *   *

Down at the bottom of the garden, behind the compost heap, Zoe, her tongue firmly pinioned between her teeth for maximum concentration, opened the back of the camera and inserted the film which she had bought the day before when they went out shopping with Maria. Chloe and Hannah, lightly flushed, leaned towards her, breathing heavily to assist. She closed the back of the camera, and wound it on until the number one appeared in the little window, just as Daddy had shown her.

'There,' she said. 'Now all we have to do is wait. You sit there, Chlo, and you sit there, Han, and I'll sit here. You've got to keep absolutely still and quiet,' she added sternly, 'or they won't come. Like with the birds at the bird table.'

Fortunately for Zoe, having regard to the likelihood of her sisters' being able to sit absolutely still and quiet for any length of time, the fairies were much less shy than the blue tits. After only a few moments there came the high-pitched buzzing which had attracted their attention to the bottom of the garden in the first place, and the first shimmering, iridescent thing appeared as if from nowhere and landed on the side of the compost heap, soon to be followed by three more.

Chloe and Hannah drew deep, satisfied breaths, and watched, entranced into stillness. Zoe lifted the camera and tried to centre the viewfinder on the group. It was hard, because they quivered and jittered so much. They were winged like large dragonflies, with the same long, narrow double wings which iridesced gold and green and blue in the bright sunshine. The wings were about two inches across, from tip to tip, and between them the narrow body hung, a little shorter, perhaps an inch and a half long. With her naked eye, Zoe could see them clearly, but in the viewfinder they were disappointingly small and vague, so clutching the camera carefully, she began to inch closer.

The bodies of the creatures seemed to glow too, though differently from the wings, with a yellow-white light which seemed to pulse slightly, like a heartbeat. They had pointed little faces with beady eyes, and long arms and legs, and they buzzed all the time, a sound like a high-pitched mosquito whine, though whether it came from the vibration of the wings or from the creatures themselves was impossible to tell.

Zoe wriggled cautiously closer, and Chloe and Hannah, breathing stertorously, copied her in every gesture. The fairies did not seem to pay any heed to the careful movements, and Zoe was soon only two feet away, and was able to see what they were doing.

They're feeding, she thought in pleased

surprise. They were digging their hands into the side of the compost heap, and drawing out what would be to them chunks of matter, and munching at them greedily, balancing on their tiny toes and vibrating their wings at incredible speed above them. She lifted the camera again and took a photograph, wound the film on, and took another, and another, as the group changed position on the heap. Then Hannah's face suddenly appeared in the viewfinder as a white cliff, and Zoe lowered the camera to frown at her. But Hannah was staring at the creatures no longer in delight, but in disgust.

'It's the do-do's,' she said in outrage. 'They're eating the do-do's!'

It was perfectly true, Zoe realised at the same moment. What the fairies were digging out and devouring so avidly were fibrous lumps of the horse-manure which their father purchased from the nearby riding-stable and so carefully spread in layers amongst the garden rubbish, kitchen refuse, and grass-cuttings.

Zoe, Chloe and Hannah had been deeply offended when they first understood whence sprang the vegetables which played so large a part in their diet. Daddy had explained that horse-manure was really clean stuff, because horses only ate grass and hay, and when rotted down with the rest of the compost it made good food for the garden; but the girls were unconvinced, and found it hard not to regard a home-grown bean or carrot with loathing. It wasn't natural, Chloe averred, and at Maria's house turned with relief and gratitude towards nice clean packets and tins, and McDonalds which you could be sure had never been anywhere near nasty dirty old horse-pooh.

And now here were the fairies doing something so gross and disgusting that all three sisters drew back from them in revulsion.

'Nasty things!' Hannah cried out tearfully, her world reeling. It was as if Postman Pat had kicked his cat. 'Nasty dirty things!' And she jerked out an arm to swat the nearest fairy.

All four rose into the air, their buzzing rising a pitch to an infuriated whine. For a moment they whirled, and then they attacked, one darting at Chloe and one at Zoe, the other two diving for Hannah. For a fraction of a second Zoe saw the little shining thing close up, saw the narrow, shrewish face, the over-large mouth with the numerous, forward-jutting, pointed teeth, and the needle-point, bright eyes; saw the naked body pulsing with the light which seemed to be shining out through the skin, as though it concealed a tiny flame inside its belly. Then she jumped back and out of the way in an instinctive movement generated by fear.

Her sisters too, sprang away, and were flailing their arms in panic, just like that time they had gone on a picnic with Mummy and Daddy and been beset by wasps. Zoe dropped the camera and looked about her for a weapon, grabbed a piece of wood which had been used in the winter as a duckboard, and swiped at the brilliant, buzzing nuisances. She heard Hannah cry out in pain and fear, and then they were all three running for the house.

'It bit me, it bit me!' Hannah screamed, abandoned with terror, and bellowed for her mother. Zoe grabbed Chloe's arm, and they stopped to take in the situation. They were not being pursued, but Hannah had run in through the French windows to the room where their mother was working, and they heard her voice, made penetrating by panic and anger, crying, 'The dirty little shit-eater bit me!'

At once there followed the sharp, percussive ring of a slap.

'We'd better go and get the camera,' said Zoe, 'or we'll be in even more trouble.'

When they finally sidled into the house, they found Hannah and Cathy in the kitchen, the latter bathing the former's arm with Dettol and water.

'What happened?' Cathy demanded, frowning. 'What was it stung her? Is there a wasps' nest down there? I'd have thought you'd know better than to let her play around with it, Zoe. You're supposed to look after your little sisters. And where did she pick up that language? Poor little Hanny-pops, did it hurt you, darling? Did the nasty wasp hurt you?'

Hannah's face was tracked with tears, her nose still red and her lip still trembling. On her forearm the puncture-mark was surrounded by a puffy, angry-looking swelling. 'Wasn't a wasp,' Hannah insisted in a quavering voice, 'and it was eating do-do's, Mummy, really it was.'

'I've brought the camera back, Mummy,' Zoe said, thinking it time to change the subject and gain some credit. She and Chloe had paused outside to remove the film and rub the casing over with the inside of Chloe's shirt so that it presented a pristine appearance. But Cathy was examining Hannah's wound and was not to be sidetracked.

'Was it a wasp?' she insisted. Zoe silenced her sisters with a look. There was no point in bringing down more wrath by mentioning the fairies.

'It was a sort of insect,' she said carefully. 'Big, with wings. Not a wasp.'

'I wonder if I'd better take you to see Dr Wrigley, my pet,' Cathy said anxiously. 'It does look awfully angry. Does it still hurt?'

'Sort of stings,' Hannah said. Cathy dabbed it again with the Dettol. She had not finished the envelopes yet.

'I think it's going down. We'll wait and see a bit. We don't want to bother Dr Wrigley unless we have to, do we?'

*   *   *

110

The photographs were a disappointment. The next day the children handed in the film at the Speediprint shop in the High Street when they were out with Maria, who promised to pick it up for them later on. She gave the yellow envelope to them on the following day, along with the credit issued by Speediprint for the eighteen unexposed frames. The six prints showed the compost heap, out of focus, with various unidentifiable, blurred masses in the background, and where the fairies should have been, only rough whited-out patches, as if drops of bleach had been splashed on the paper.

'Overexposed. What a shame,' said Maria, who had no idea what the girls had been trying to photograph. 'Never mind,' she said consolingly. 'We'll stop at McDonalds for lunch on our way home, shall we?'

'Yippee!' cried Zoe and Chloe. 'Can we have milkshakes, too?'

Hannah said nothing. She had been a little quiet and pale all day.

Maria bought them all hamburgers and milkshakes and they settled round a table in a corner and unwrapped and attacked the goodies with relish. Immediately the peace was ruptured by a cry of disgust from Hannah, who spat her first mouthful violently onto the table-top, and sat spluttering and bellowing, clawing angrily at her lips and tongue with her fingers like a monkey who had just bitten a chilli.

'Yeuch! Nasty! Nasty!' she cried, salivating and spitting juicily onto the table. Zoe and Chloe had drawn back with fastidious cries, and Maria, torn between anger at Hannah's table manners and concern over what might have been wrong with the food, tried to restore order, conduct a post-mortem, and field the enquiries of the under-manager who came over to see what the trouble was. In the midst of the confusion, the under-manager laid a hand on Hannah's shoulder, and his murmur of 'Poor little girl!' terminated in a yell as the poor little girl in question whipped her head round with surprising speed and bit him.

'Ow! Wow! You little beast!' The under-manager, doing a fair imitation of an ethnic fertility dance, shook his injured hand, and bright spots of blood flew from pairs of puncture wounds. He examined them with horror and amazement. 'She must have teeth like an alligator,' he cried, looking at Hannah with loathing. 'You ought to keep her muzzled.' And Hannah, grinning at him maliciously, displayed teeth which suddenly did look oddly sharp and crowded in her small mouth.

*   *   *

'I'm awfully worried about her,' Cathy confided to Andrew over their pre-dinner gin-

and-tonics in the large, farmhouse-style kitchen that evening. Andrew, who had changed out of his 'work' suit into freshly-pressed Levi jeans, Gucci shirt, and a pair of leather espadrilles, liked to relax at the scrubbed wooden table sipping his drink and glancing through the evening paper while Cathy stood at the stove waiting for the vegetables to finish.

'Hmm?' he said.

'She's been awfully quiet, and she didn't eat a thing at supper.'

'Hmm,' said Andrew, turning a page.

'I wonder if she mightn't have some kind of infection.'

'Hmm?'

'You know, from that sting the other night. Or an allergic reaction. She looked feverish to me, though she didn't feel hot, and her forehead was quite cool.'

'Hmm.'

'I felt her forehead, and you know, just for a moment—' she laughed nervously at her own folly, 'just for a moment I was afraid she was going to bite me!'

'Surely not,' Andrew murmured, reading his stars. '*Conflicts on the domestic scene will be ironed out smoothly if you exercise your usual tact and charm. A letter may bring surprising news about a partnership or joint venture . . .*'

'Oh, I know it's silly but—' Cathy sighed. 'It isn't like her to be so naughty. And she loves

113

McDonalds. They all do.'

Andrew looked up, his eyes wide with amazement. He laid down his newspaper and stared at his wife. 'What did you just say?' he demanded slowly.

Cathy wasn't sure which bit he wanted repeating. 'I just think she's not herself,' she offered. Andrew's face suffused with growing wrath.

'You said something about McDonalds,' he said dangerously. 'Am I to understand that you allowed my children to patronise a hamburger house?'

'Well,' Cathy said nervously, caught on the wrong foot, 'Maria does take them sometimes. But only occasionally, as a special treat.'

'A treat?'

'Oh—well—you know what children are!' Cathy smiled feebly. 'You spend your life trying to get them to appreciate the finer things in life, and they still insist on preferring junk.'

'You let the childminder feed my children on junk food?' Andrew said wrathfully, being, Cathy thought, painfully slow about it. 'After all the hours I've spent in the garden, growing healthy, organic vegetables, and going miles out of my way to get free-range eggs and unpasteurised milk from the farm. Don't you realise what you're doing to them? The habits they learn at this age will stay with them for the rest of their lives, and if you allow them to think of that filthy junk food as a treat—'

'But they do,' Cathy cried in her defence. 'It's nothing to do with me. I didn't teach them to like hamburgers and chips—they just do, naturally.'

'Naturally?'

'And they don't like raw vegetables,' she went on bravely, 'and the fact that the veggies are grown from horse-manure upsets them. They were playing on the compost heap when this insect or whatever it was stung Hannah, and—'

'My compost heap!' With a yelp, her husband had bolted from the table, out of the kitchen door, and down the garden. 'You let the children play on my compost heap!'

Cathy ran after him, abandoning the supper vegetables to their fate. At the bottom of the garden, Andrew found the compost heap undamaged by childish ravages, despite the fact that Hannah, in her Snowman pyjamas, and hungry from her missed supper, had slipped out of the house and was standing beside it, digging out firm, friable lumps of horse-manure and chomping them voraciously.

As her father rushed up to her, she bared her narrow, sharp-pointed teeth at him, and a cloud of strange, glowing insects rose from the heap and whirled about him, with a high-pitched whining buzz, which reminded Andrew of the mosquitoes which had made his and Cathy's honeymoon in the Camargue such a

115

misery.

It must have been that memory, he reflected afterwards, which had made him lose his temper. He plunged in with a yell, slapped Hannah so hard she was too surprised to cry, and practically flung her at her mother, with the command to put her to bed at once. Then he ran next door to the Simpsons, dragging Bill Simpson away from *Eastenders* and demanding to borrow his garden insecticide spray. Running back to his own garden, he sprayed and sprayed and sprayed the heap until the last of the revolting little shining insects had fallen writhing to the ground. And even then, he stamped on the bodies, practically dancing on them until there was not a vestige of them to be seen, and he was out of breath and suddenly sobered with embarrassment at his own behaviour.

'You should have stopped me,' he said afterwards reproachfully to his wife. The reverberations went on for days. 'It's against all our principles to use chemical insecticides. And, after all our hard work, that heap's ruined now. All that lovely organic compost, contaminated with laboratory poisons.'

Cathy couldn't help feeling he was being unreasonable in blaming her, and they quarrelled, as she confided to Maria over a cup of camomile tea one day later that week when Maria brought the children back.

'And to make it worse, Bill next door has

been congratulating him over the fence for seeing the light at last as far as sprays are concerned. He always complained our garden was a greenfly's paradise, and that he suffered for our prejudices.' She sighed. 'Life's so unfair.'

Maria made sympathetic murmurings, and then, to take her employer's mind off her troubles, told her the latest juicy titbit of gossip, about how the under-manager of the McDonalds in the High Street had been sacked for jumping over the counter and biting a young female customer, who had simply asked him for two Big Macs, a cheeseburger, and three large chips to take away.

LONELY IN A STRANGER'S HOUSE

LONELY IN A STRANGER'S HOUSE

Love came late to me, though I was married at twenty.

I don't now remember why Jim and I married. We were both twenty, thought we knew everything, thought we loved each other and would never change. Childhood seemed so far behind us. We were mature adults now. In some ways, twenty is the oldest age of all.

Well, we married and set up house together. Though ambitious, I was always a womanly woman and I believed in love and marriage and children. I cooked and washed and cleaned and sewed; hunted out bargains, balanced the budget, paid the bills; looked after Jim, cared for Jim and tried to make him comfortable. I managed to hold down a job at the same time and to add something every month to our savings. Wasn't I clever? Jim said so, but it didn't seem to make him happy.

So we decided to have a baby. I had always assumed that having a baby was the most straightforward thing in the world. It was what we were for, wasn't it? We both came from large families. I'd be pregnant in no time.

It took five years. The doctors said there was nothing wrong with either of us so we tried not to worry, but every month I wasn't pregnant made me more determined. I *would* have a baby. Besides, Jim wasn't happy. I was making him unhappy by not giving him children, wasn't I? So I must have a baby for Jim's sake, too.

It happened at last, and then it was all easy. I loved being pregnant. I sang about the house, talked to dogs and babies in the street, and bought flowers on the way home from work to make the house look cheerful. Jim was happy too. We planned things together, and went shopping together. Suddenly we had plenty to say to each other, and I realised how little we had talked over the past year.

Labour started. I said goodbye to Jim, who was going off to work, and took myself off to hospital. (In the bad old days, fathers weren't allowed to watch.) 'I'll be in and out in no time,' I told him. 'I'll be home with the baby before you are tonight.'

Something went wrong. Hours passed and there was a world of pain but nothing coming of it; pain blurring into fog through which figures moved dimly, half-perceived. Then a face hanging over me.

'We'll have to do a Caesarian, Mrs Jones.'

'No,' I said, but nobody heard me.

'Just a little prick, Mrs Jones, and then you'll have a lovely sleep.'

'No,' I said, but they didn't listen.

They got me with the needle, and black pillows surged up to smother me. I was not to be present at my own child's birth. I was not to

122

be allowed that privilege.

They told me, the first thing when I woke, that there would never be another. The damage, they said, was too great. It would be too dangerous. In my own interests, they said, they had fixed it so that I couldn't conceive again. (In the bad old days, they did things like that.)

But never mind, we had one child—a girl—and when they finally let me see her, let me hold her in my arms, I didn't mind about anything else.

Jim was allowed in to see me, and they let him hold the baby. What can compare with that moment? His face was transfixed with joy. Had I done that for him? I felt so humble and so proud.

We called her Mary: no other name seemed important enough for so unique a creature. She was beautiful, and intelligent, and we loved her.

So now I had more things to be good at: a home and husband to run, a child to rear and, pretty soon, a job to hold down as well. I managed it all. Wasn't I clever? Jim didn't say so this time, but then he was hardly ever home. He had to work longer hours, because whichever way you look at it, babies cost money.

But Jim loved Mary, and on Saturdays and Sundays she was all his. She loved him more than me, but I didn't mind—I swear it! Little girls have to love their fathers. That's how they learn to love a man. And if that love goes wrong, sometimes they lose heart and never try again. So I never minded when he took her away at weekends to the park, the zoo or the river. It gave me time to do things of my own, and they both looked so happy when they came home, full of the things they had seen and done.

For seven more years I cooked and cleaned and washed and ironed. I shopped and paid the bills and balanced the budget—and I never noticed all that time that I was alone. Do you understand what I mean? Yes, you do. It happens to so many of us.

Then one day Mary was a little ailing. Nothing much, just a little hot and fractious. The next day she was plainly sickening for something; the next day they took her into hospital. It all happened so quickly, and a fog of pain and disbelief blurs the memory. But by Friday she was dead. It was as quick as that. She was snatched from us before we knew it, and on Saturday when we woke we didn't know what to do with ourselves.

'I was going to take her skating,' Jim said. He said it often that day, hurt and indignant, as though someone would realise they'd been unfair and bring her back.

We aren't meant to outlive our children. The nature in us sickens and fails at so monstrous a reversal. I have known women, both before and since, who have simply died of bewilderment. Oh, they still walked and talked as though they were alive, but they were only waiting for time to catch up with them and make them lie down.

It didn't kill me—I was too strong—oh, but nearly, nearly!

I didn't notice that Jim was fading from me. He had been so little with me in any case that I didn't notice him growing transparent. He wasn't a cruel man. He had love to give, but he couldn't give it to me. When we lost Mary, he turned away from me and found someone else, a younger woman with no scars and no bruises.

And now I was really alone.

There followed empty years. I was strong, I was sensible, so I didn't stay at home and brood. I had my job: a career, with my own office at home. I had a social life, I had friends—even male friends. There were men who were attracted to me, and some even tried to love me. I tried to love them back, truly I did. Sometimes I even thought I had succeeded, and wept a little when it was over, but it was only on the surface. The nature of me was buried, and buried deep. Not dead, oh no! They were not dead years, but fallow. It was a winter, and in winter things don't die, but lie inert until the sun warms the soil again.

One day spring came, quite suddenly. It was a Saturday, and I was struggling home with loaded carrier bags. One bag split, and in making a grab for my purchases I dropped the rest, and my shopping was strewn over the pavement. Such a little mishap—why then, did I burst into tears? Why did I weep in public as though for a lost child?

But then John was there, picking up the pieces. 'Don't worry, I've got a spare bag here. Nothing's broken. It's all right.'

Was it? I thought; and then I saw that it was.

He helped me carry everything home. 'You must have a large family, to buy so much.'

'No, it's for a dinner party tonight,' I said, and then, surprising myself, I asked, 'Will you come?'

He arrived early, as I hoped he would. I opened the door to him, and felt so glad, just at the sight of him. The door stuck a little, as it always did.

'Have you a plane, or a chisel?' he asked. 'I can fix that for you now.'

He fixed it. At dinner he opened the wine and kept the conversation going. When everyone had gone he washed up while I dried, and even did the saucepans and wiped the top of the gas stove, the things men forget. 'I've lived alone for eight years,' he explained. 'You get used to doing these things.'

He was in my life. Had there ever been a time when hc was not?

'I'll come round tomorrow and fix that tap for you,' he said.

'You needn't,' I said.

'But I want to.'

'Why?' I asked.

'Because I care about you,' he said.

He worked just round the corner from me, ten minutes' walk away. Oh, that was a good year! The days we didn't have lunch together were rare, grey days. I sang over the washing up, talked to dogs and children in the street, and bought flowers so often I ran out of vases. Hours, days and months together, never a moment wasted. I hardly had time to warn myself to beware, to tell myself it couldn't last. It *felt* as though it would last. I couldn't imagine life without him.

Until one day he said, 'My job is moving to Newcastle. I have to go.'

I said nothing. I kept very still. Have you seen a field mouse when an owl's shadow crosses the moon? This was the end. The tender, green shoots I had put forth would be frost-nipped, would wither. I had not been careful. I had not held back and warned myself that nothing lasts. I had started to come alive, and being alive hurts.

'Marry me,' he said. 'Come with me.'

Who would say no? Not even I said no, but I couldn't say yes. I thought of the risks. To leave my house, my career, my friends, my town, and go to a strange place with a man whom, let's face it, I hardly knew? To give up my independence and place my fortunes in another's hands? To leave my single state and marry—that hazardous undertaking—and who knew if it would work? He might leave me, and what then? To be lonely in my own house was one thing, and bad enough, but to be lonely in a stranger's house would be desolation.

Then I found I wasn't strong. No more clever me. 'I'm afraid,' I said.

How can I praise this man? What words would be enough? A lesser man would have said, 'Afraid of what?' A lesser man would have said, 'Don't be silly.' A lesser man would have said, 'That's a nice thing to say when I've just proposed to you!'

But he only touched my head, as a man touches a child, to care for it and protect it; a touch that gives trust as much as it invites it. 'Marry me,' he said. 'I can't be whole without you.'

I saw I had been foolish. The risks were his risks too. How could I ever be alone, when we even shared the same dangers?

I was still afraid, but I said yes.

And then love came to me.

SUITABLE

SUITABLE

The corridors of the Admiralty building were always cradled in a seemly hush, as befitted such a venerable institution as the Royal Space Navy, with its roots deep in tradition. Even so, on the nineteenth floor, where the Admiral of the Fleet and the Secretary to the First Lord had their offices, the atmosphere was almost holy.

Martin certainly felt it so as he waited for the answer to his knock on the dark blue door with the gleaming brass fittings. The walls of the corridor were painted a subtle, soothing grey, the carpeted floor was a slightly darker grey, and the doors stood out in handsome contrast—handsome and forbidding. It would take a bold man to knock, who had no appointment.

Martin had an appointment. In its honour, he had put on fresh overalls, agreeably crisp with starch, and ironed as smooth as his well-shaven chin. Below the blue and-gold epaulettes of the Space Navy, his overalls were maintenance-technician grey—the same colour as the walls. From his long and intimate acquaintance with stores returns, Martin was aware that that particular shade was called Battleship Grey, a stirring reference to the historic days of the sea-going navy. Naval

131

history was a compulsory part of the RSN induction course, but Martin, from personal interest, had read more widely than the curriculum, and his mind was furnished with many a recondite fact, his imagination replete with a number of thrilling and obsolete words like frigate and ironclad and ship-of-the-line.

He had often pondered the psychological significance of the fact that his overalls and the walls were the same colour. No doubt those in authority over him would say it was a compliment, suggesting that the maintenance man was so essential to a ship that he could be considered part of its fabric. Martin, however, had a different theory. It was intended as camouflage. If the lowly maintenance technician could be made to blend into the background, the eyes of senior officers need not be offended by the sight of him.

His knock was answered, and Martin entered the sanctum sanctorum. His nostrils twitched as they caught the scent of undiluted power. He tried to move smartly, but the depth of the carpet pile defeated him, slowing him to a complete halt at an appropriate distance inside the door. He wondered vaguely if it had been calculated so. At the far side of the vast mahogany desk, the Admiral looked up and gave him a civil smile.

'Martin, isn't it? Yes, come in, come in. Do sit down. Now, what can I do for you?'

In the new democratic Space Navy, anyone,

however insignificant, had access to the most senior officer, without being required to explain their business to an intermediary. All that was required was an appointment. Of course, by rationing appointments and setting them ludicrously far ahead, the system ensured that only the most determined finally got to waste the Commander-in-Chief's time.

Martin had waited eighteen months for this moment, and was aware that his five minutes would be sandwiched between other business of the gravest importance, strategic problems and policy decisions that could affect the whole galaxy. The knowledge did not overawe him. In his view, his business was as vital and fundamental to the Service as anything else the Admiral would consider that day—though he had no doubt that the Admiral wouldn't think so.

Martin took the proffered chair and assembled his thoughts, while the Admiral, hands resting relaxedly on the desk-top, gave him at least the appearance of complete attention. Reputation said this particular Admiral of the Fleet had risen to the paramount position through skill in handling people and meticulous preparation for every meeting. The personal assistant would have called up Martin's record and, doubtless knowing quite well why he had requested the appointment, would have given the Admiral a complete run-down. It was therefore tactless in the extreme for her to address him by his Christian name.

'Maintenance Technician First Class Davidson, Ma'am,' he said evenly, meeting her eye. She inclined her head slightly, which might have been an acknowledgement of the correction, or may simply have indicated her continuing attention. 'It's about my application for admission to the Flying Officer's Training Course, Ma'am.'

She gestured with one hand towards the buff folder lying on the desk before her. 'Your third application,' she said with a faint, wry smile.

'It was turned down,' he said baldly. 'I'd like to know why.'

He thought she sighed as she folded her hands together and leaned forward a little to address him across the desk.

'You know very well why,' she said. 'Men are not admitted to that course.'

'I have all the preliminary qualifications,' he said rigidly, keeping himself on a tight rein. 'I have the technical skills, the appropriate medical certificates, and more than the minimum service requirement.'

'Indeed,' she agreed genially. 'You are very well qualified. Perhaps over-qualified for your present position. But men are not admitted to the Flying Officer's Training Course. Men cannot be spaceship pilots.'

Martin's hands, resting on his knees, balled

134

of their own volition into fists. 'Will you explain to me why, Ma'am?'

'Oh come on, Martin, you know very well why. Must we go over all this again? Men simply aren't suitable material for deep space pilots, either physically or temperamentally.'

'Surely that's a question of individual character, Ma'am, rather than any gender-related difference,' Martin said.

'Not in our experience,' the Admiral said. 'All our studies show that men can't stand the strain of long space-flights. They get tense, irritable, and aggressive, and then they make mistakes. And you don't need me to tell you that you can't afford mistakes out there.'

'Men used to fly aeroplanes. In fact it was men who pioneered flying in the first place.'

'Yes, and look at the mistakes they made, and the terrible accidents and loss of life that ensued. We can't risk that out in space. Come now, Martin, no one blames you. It's a hormonal thing. Men are different from women, and that's all there is to it.' She got up and came round the desk, and perched herself on the corner of it, smiling down at him kindly. Her handsome face, lined with authority and responsibility, softened to an expression of sympathy which Martin believed to be wholly artificial. He resisted it.

'Men aren't different from women in any way that matters,' he insisted passionately.

'Oh, you don't really believe that,' she

coaxed. 'After all, you only have to look in the mirror. You men have big, strong bodies and big, strong muscles, and you were made that way for a purpose. Pulling things and lifting things, that's what you're good at—and thank heaven for it! It's nothing to be ashamed of, Martin. There's a right place for everyone in society. You just concentrate on doing what you're good at, and leave us to worry about space flight. Besides,' she leaned forward and patted Martin's leg, and her fingers seemed to linger appreciatively upon his well-muscled thigh, 'a good-looking boy like you, with your splendid physique—in a year or two you'll be on a breeding programme, and then you'll have better things to think about than nasty old spaceships.'

Martin felt himself blushing with anger and vexation. He held himself rigidly aloof and said stiffly, 'Thank you, Ma'am, but I'm not interested in breeding.'

She laughed genially. 'Oh, you say that now, but you'll change your mind when the time comes. It's Nature! All men like breeding. And a good thing for all of us that they do, or what would become of the human race, eh? And now,' she stood up and assumed the mantle of briskness, 'I'm afraid I'll have to ask you to run along. I'm a very busy woman, as I'm sure you understand.'

He stood, and she ushered him to the door and opened it for him courteously. 'I'm glad we've had this little talk,' she said. 'I think it's sorted out one or two things.'

He found himself outside in the hushed grey corridor, and the door closed gently, but firmly, behind him. Burning with frustration, he retraced his steps, took the service lift and descended the nineteen floors to the maintenance depot in the basement—his rightful place, he thought savagely. Know your place, that's what they said; and a man's place is in the basement, for ever and ever, amen.

He hated the depot, with its 'masculine' colour scheme and homely touches—chunky furniture, blinds at the window instead of curtains, framed prints of veteran cars and motorcycles on the walls—all designed to keep them contented and acquiescent in their lot. Recently all the trolleys had been fitted with 'number plates' like old-style ground-cars, and you were supposed to get deeply attached to your own personal trolley and take a pride in it. Women, he reflected savagely, thought all men were obsessed with machinery.

He pushed moodily through the rubber-faced swing doors, and his friend Jamie, loading his trolley at the hatch, looked up with an enquiring lift of the eyebrows.

'How did it go, then?'

'How d'you think?' Martin said shortly. He stumped across the room to where his own trolley was parked up against the rechargers, and whirled the combination lock irritably. 'All the usual old rubbish about men not being suitable. "It's your hormones, dear".' He pitched his voice in a savage falsetto. '"You just go on shifting heavy weights, and don't worry your handsome head about nasty old spaceships". Smug, patronising bitch! God, it makes me sick!'

'Well, you must have known what she was going to say before you went,' said Jamie reasonably. 'I don't know why you go on banging your head against a brick wall, Mart. We do all right, don't we? We get decent pay, we've got the sports club, and the work isn't hard. What more do you want?'

'Fine help you are,' Martin said crossly. 'And do you know what the final insult was? She told me in a year or two I'd be breeding, and then I wouldn't care about being a pilot any more. Breeding! That's always their excuse. As if all men simply lived and breathed to get on a breeding programme!'

'Well, most of us do,' Jamie shrugged. 'I'm certainly looking forward to it, anyway. Why not? Any normal man would. It's only natural.'

'You sound just like her,' Martin retorted.

Jamie braced himself and swung his laden trolley round and lined it up with the doors. 'I dunno about that,' he said calmly. 'But I'll tell you one thing—I wouldn't fancy taking a trip on a spaceship if I knew it was a man flying it.' And whistling cheerfully, he shoved his trolley through the doors and out into the corridor.

138

Martin watched him go, his shoulders hunched morosely.

'Men like you do more harm to the men's cause than women ever do!' he shouted after him. 'We're our own worst enemies.'

LOVING MEMORY

LOVING MEMORY

It would be too extreme to say that Prue rejoiced at the news of Dad's death, but there was a sort of grim satisfaction, all the same, in the fact that Mum had finally outlived him.

All the way down on the train the rattling of the wheels was a harsh counterpoint to her harsher memories of him: loud-voiced, brutally-spoken, bad-tempered. Not in a natural, sparked-off, quickly-over way, but brooding, gathering, self-propagating. Dad was proud of his bad temper, stroked it, stoked it up, unleashed it as a man might unleash a fighting-dog, and there was somehow something obscene about his satisfaction when he had reduced Mum to quivering tears.

Not that he ever hit her, or any of the girls, though he 'thrashed' the boys, claiming they 'needed it'. His eyes would grow small, and the veins would begin to stand out on his bald head, and he would say in that horrible, gloating voice, 'Right, I know what you need! You need a bloody good thrashing—and by God I'm going to see you get it!'

It didn't matter too much when he hit Bob Bob was tough. He simply shrugged it off, and by the time he was fourteen he had grown so big and muscular that when Dad started on him he would simply eye him speculatively, as if inviting the opportunity to try his young muscles against Dad's middle-aged ones. Soon after that Dad gave up thrashing Bob, and even moderated his language when Bob was around. But Bob left home the moment he was legally entitled to, so he wasn't much help to the rest of them.

But Kim was another matter. Kim was shy and sensitive, and his terror of his father only seemed to give Dad more enjoyment out of the situation, and lead to more beatings than Bob had ever endured. Often and often Mum would try to shield Kim, but it never did any good. Dad would drag him out from behind Mum's skirts, and hook his head under his arm, and thrash him while Mum quivered and wept silently.

Prue found her hands sweating and her fingernails digging into her palms, and forced herself to relax them. He had made her childhood hell, and she hated him so much that the memories of him were still vivid, even though she, like Bob, had made her escape into the wide world when she was seventeen, and vowed never to go back. She had gone back sometimes, for Mum's sake, and had found the tyrant smaller than she remembered, but just as hateful, shrinking and hardening with age, but still bellowing, glaring around him with his little, savage, mean-tempered eyes, like a bull's, and whipping himself into a rage for the sheer pleasure of it.

144

His end, she thought, was just what one would have predicted for him. Remembering how the veins used to bulge on his temples, how his face used to congest with temper, it was only to be expected that he should die, in the end, of a stroke. He had died in the outside privy—another of his idiosyncrasies being that he would not use the inside loo. He went every morning at the same time down the garden, carrying his newspaper and cigarettes, and spending half an hour in the dark, earth-smelling closet, round which the stinging-nettles grew so tall and lush, pressing right up to the walls as though trying to get closer to one they recognised as their true master.

'Communing with nature', he called it, with an arch humour that did not invite smiles. And woe betide anyone who disturbed him, intentionally or unintentionally, while he communed. That was why, as Kim explained in his letter, it had taken so long to discover him. Mum had tried to explain to the doctor, and then to the policeman, that it simply wasn't possible to go down there and tap on the door and ask if he was all right, even when he had been gone nearly two hours. His death, Pru thought, befitted him: it was solitary and angry, it was irony and obscenity. She wished there were some way he could have been left there, that the privy could have been his coffin and his mausoleum. It was certainly, she thought, a fitting monument.

*   *   *

The train pulled in at Hurstfield station, and Prue got out, by now thoroughly churned up inside, feeling as sick and apprehensive as she always had arriving here when Dad was alive. Out of the station, down the lane, turn left at the post office, and second right, a walk of eight minutes' duration. The station was eight minutes away from the hell of random offence. Eight minutes before he might leap out at her and bellow about something that had not been a sin the day before, would not be a sin the day after. The unpredictability, that was what was so unendurable—and of course he knew it, the old sadist.

Maddy and Kim were waiting for her. 'I've got the car outside,' Maddy said, kissing her cheek. Her hair was grey all over now, and she had permed it, which made her look twenty years older than she was.

'The car!' Prue heard her voice creak like something long unused. 'We'll be home too soon.' She needed time to prepare herself.

'It's all right now,' Kim said, understanding her. There were dark shadows like bruises under his eyes, but he still looked to her delicate and pretty, as if he should really have been a girl. Was that why Dad had hated him so? She put her arms round him and he returned her hug fiercely. He had always been

146

her particular pet.

'How's Mum taking it?' Prue asked.

'Oh, you know Mum,' Maddy said unhelpfully.

'Quietly,' Kim told her. 'I don't think she's really taken it in yet.'

They walked outside into the sunshine. Maddy's old Volkswagen Beetle sat by the grass verge quietly rusting. Maddy went round to the driver's door, and then paused, leaning against the roof, picking absently at a paint blister. 'I can't help thinking,' she began.

'Don't, Mad,' Kim said quickly.

'No, but really—it was so long before she called anyone. He'd been dead over an hour, Dr Ross said.'

'Don't, Maddy.'

'But suppose,' she said stubbornly, looking up. Her eyes were frightened. 'He might have been dying, calling out, banging on the door for help. She might have heard him. Maybe she heard him, and didn't go.' Large, terrible fears gathered in Maddy's eyes, like the shadows of sharks in blue water. 'I keep thinking about it. I keep seeing him in there, dying—'

Kim went round to her and put his arm over her shoulders. Prue could only look on, helplessly. She had thought the same things. Maddy turned her face to Kim's shoulder, too rigid to fit the shape of his comforting. 'I keep thinking he's going to come back and punish

147

us for letting him die,' she said.

Kim met Prue's gaze, and they read the same fear in each other's eyes. But he spoke briskly and matter-of-factly. 'Don't be silly, Mad. He's dead. He can't come back. He can't hurt any of us ever again.'

*   *   *

The house was full of people, her brothers and sisters and their spouses and children; aunts, uncles and cousins, who seemed to emerge from the obscurity of oblivion only for family funerals; neighbours looked embarrassed at being caught out of context; friends of Mum's from All Saints where she had done the flowers for twenty-five years. The universal features of all funerals were there, the black dresses and ties, the shiny shoes, the helpful cousins chatting in the kitchen as they unpacked sausage rolls from Tupperware boxes and cut sandwiches for 'afterwards', the unnaturally clean children dashing in from the garden demanding drinks.

The phone rang and Aunty Cath poked her head round the door for Gwenny, saying, 'It's about the flowers, love, only I don't want to bother your mum.' The kettle boiled continuously on the gas stove, and the kitchen smelled of hot discarded tea-leaves as pot after pot of tea was made and distributed. A grey old man who didn't seem to belong to anyone made himself useful collecting up the empty cups and carrying them to the kitchen, smiling proudly at everyone with gleaming false teeth that had surely been made for someone else, they seemed much too big for him.

And there was Mum at last, in the sitting-room, standing by the empty fireplace, with Bob on one side and Sibby on the other, as if they expected to have to hold her up. Prue's heart contracted with love. Mum looked so tiny, fragile and mouse-coloured. A small woman, narrow rather than thin, with soft hair, soft skin and soft eyes, with a hesitant, placatory smile for everyone. But she had outlived him, the foul, bellowing tyrant, Prue thought in triumph. She had seen him off, and now she was going to bury him, and live the rest of her life breathing deeply and easily without fear.

'Hullo, Mum!' Prue said diffidently, and went to embrace her. Mum returned the hug calmly, smiling a vague welcome.

'Hullo, love. Good journey? Ingrid phoned up to say her train's been cancelled, she's going to be late. I hope she manages to get here in time. Everyone else has come, even Aunty Irene. She came down last night, but she stayed in Eastbury. She said she didn't want to put me out.'

She sounded so normal, Prue thought in astonishment, as the gentle, commonplace voice trickled on. She met Bob's eyes, Bob who

149

towered above them all, who looked so like Dad, except that it was a Dad made human and warm. Bob who had escaped, too, and made good, out in the real world where action and consequence were linked by logic, and life was so very, very simple.

'She's been chattering like a budgie for hours,' he said, putting an affectionate arm round Mum. 'It takes different people different ways. But she's all right, aren't you, Mum?'

'Of course, dear,' she said, sounding mildly surprised. Sibby mouthed at Prue, 'She hasn't taken it in yet.' It was to be expected. At the graveside, that's when it would come home to her. What would she do then—turn somersaults? Burst into laughter? Prue regarded her mother in amazement, that such a frail, pallid creature could have borne seven children—five girls and two boys—and lived forty years with a sadistic bully, yet show so little sign of it.

*   *   *

He was being buried at All Saints, in the churchyard, with a full Christian burial service. Gwenny said to Prue as they filed into the front pews, 'It's all wrong. Dad never went to church in his life, except on his wedding day, and he'd have stopped Mum coming if he could. Why should he have a Christian burial?

If he was a Christian, so was Hitler.'

'It's for Mum really, I suppose,' Prue said. 'These are all her friends.'

'I don't know what the vicar's going to find to say about him,' said Maddy on her other side. 'He's supposed to do one of those "what a great bloke he was and how we'll miss him" speeches. But he knows what Mum went through.'

'Ingrid hasn't arrived,' Gwenny said after a moment, looking around.

'She's not coming,' Sibby said, leaning forward from the pew behind where she sat with her husband. Of the seven of them, only Bob and Sibby had married. They had been the ones least affected by Dad, Bob because he was big and strong and got out as soon as he could, Sibby because as the youngest she had been cushioned to an extent by the older children. The middle five had remained single. Prue could never bring herself to get really close to a man—another thing to lay at Dad's door. She thought it was probably the same for the others.

'Not coming?' Gwenny said.

'She phoned me the day before yesterday,' Sibby said with a sort of grim satisfaction. 'She said she thought the whole thing was disgusting, a proper funeral for him, when we'd all hated him so much. But she didn't want to upset Mum, so she said she'd say she was coming, and then phone up and say there was trouble with the trains. She said it would choke her to hear all that stuff about his soul going to heaven. She said she knew where he was going, and she'd happily stoke the fires herself.'

'Poor Mum,' Maddy said. 'I think that's mean. She'd naturally want us all here. It's for her sake, not for Dad's.'

'But Ingrid's never visited,' Kim reminded her. 'She said when she left that she'd never come back. She never forgave him for cutting off her hair.'

'She said she'd never come back while he was alive,' Maddy corrected. 'She ought to be here now he's dead, for Mum's sake.'

*   *   *

The vicar's eulogy was a masterpiece of persiflage. It sounded good, but said absolutely nothing.

'He should have been a politician,' Kim murmured to Prue.

'Or an advertising man,' she whispered back.

They filed out to the graveside. The earth, dug out and piled up round the edges of the grave, had been covered with sheets of bright, green plastic grass, the sort you see in greengrocers' shops. The coffin, gleaming pale wood and brass fittings, rested beside it on the

152

real grass, the webbing ropes tastefully draped around it. It was a mixture of the twee and the gruesome, Prue felt, which would have upset her deeply, had it been the funeral of someone she loved. The funeral-parlour men, too, were horribly professional, pushing people into place according to a private etiquette only they understood or cared about, and standing with hands clasped before them and eyes bent in a professional sorrow which made her want to hit them.

The children ranged themselves to either side of Mum along one side of the grave, Bob, Sibby, and their families to one side, Gwenny, Maddy, Kim and Prue to the other, as the funeral-parlour men in hushed and tender voices had directed them. All those most deeply affected by the bereavement were to have ringside seats, to get the best view. If only they knew, Prue thought with vicious amusement. We're more likely to cheer as the old beast goes down than weep. We'd sooner it was a hanging than a burial, but a burial will do nicely, thank you.

No-one cried. It was a hot day, and very still except for birdsong. The vicar's voice droned pleasantly like a bee. Everyone looked somnolent. At the last moment Prue tried to find some shred of Christian forgiveness in her, even of understanding, but she had nothing except gladness that it was over, and that they could begin to live their own lives at

last, out of the shadow. He could never hurt
them again.

*   *   *

It was very late before all the friends,
neighbours and more distant relatives had
gone, and only the immediate family were left.

'So what will you do now, Vie?' Aunty Cath
asked. 'Will you sell this house? You could buy
a little place near me. There are some nice
new houses going up, down at the end of the
Shinfield Road. Town houses, they call them,
just the right size for one. I expect you'll find
this house too big now. And the garden'll be
too much for you to manage on your own.'

'Oh no, I don't think I'll move. I like it
here,' Mum said calmly. 'This is my home,
after all.'

'It was his home,' Aunty Irene corrected
shortly. 'I shouldn't have thought you'd want
to stay on.'

'Why not?' said Mum, looking round
vaguely. 'It's a nice house. I've lived here for
forty years. I wouldn't want to be uprooting
myself at my time of life. I've got all my things
around me.'

Eventually Aunty Irene and Aunty Cath
went, then Bob and Sibby had to go because of
the children, and then there was only Gwen,
Maddy, Kim and Prue left. They sat around in
the living room in silence, feeling exhausted

154

and ill at ease, unable to think of anything to say. Every thought seemed to lead back to Dad. Alive or dead, the shadow was still there. How long, how many years, would it be, before they were really out from under it?

'I think I'll make some tea,' Mum said at last. Gwen started to get up, and Mum smiled fondly at her. 'No, don't you bother, love. I'll do it.'

When she had gone, Kim said, 'Will you stay, Prue? We've made up beds. Gwenny's stopping, but she's got to go tomorrow. I don't think Mum ought to be left alone for a bit. You can see she's in a state of shock. It hasn't caught up with her yet.'

'Yes, all right,' Prue said. There was a long silence.

'And then there's all the sorting out to do,' Maddy said. 'His clothes and everything.'

'God, I couldn't,' Gwen said, shuddering. 'I couldn't touch them.'

'Someone's got to,' Kim said unhappily. 'We can't leave it all to Mum. Think how much worse it would be for her.'

'Well, Maddy ought to, then,' Gwen said. 'She's a nurse.'

'What difference does that make?' Maddy said indignantly.

'I'll help,' Prue said. Another long silence fell.

Gwen said, 'She's been gone a long time. I wonder if she's all right.'

155

Prue got up. 'I'll go and help her carry things in.'

In the kitchen the kettle was boiling. It must have been boiling for some time, for the ceiling was wreathed in steam. Mum stood by the open back door, staring out into the dark garden. Prue turned off the gas, and went to her mother; was afraid to touch her, and then put a tentative hand on her shoulder. Mum turned her head a little. Her cheeks were wet, glistening with tears.

'He loved his garden so,' Mum said. 'I can't believe I'll never see him again.'

Prue was silent, unable to find any words for what she was feeling. She had seen her mother cry so often in childhood, but then it had always made her angry.

'Everything reminds me of him,' Mum was saying, her quiet voice faded almost to nothing. 'All the things around me. Now I'll never see him again. Never bring him another cup of tea. Never hear him come in through the door.' Her voice faltered. 'I keep thinking, that there's nothing I can do to please him, ever again.'

Prue was rigid with shock, realising at last that her mother was not crying with relief, but with sorrow.

'You can't,' she said at last, swallowing a lump of dismay and betrayal. 'You can't be sorry he's gone, after the way he treated you?'

'You don't understand,' said Mum. 'I was

married to him for forty years. I was only eighteen when we got married, just a girl.'

'But you didn't love him. You couldn't, when he was so vile to you.' She had thought he couldn't hurt her any more, the old beast, but here was Mum crying for him, missing him, wanting him back, and that was the worst of all, that hurt more than anything. 'He was a monster!'

Mum's damp face crinkled up into a smile in spite of everything, and she looked to Prue, just for a moment, not like her mother at all but like a woman quite separate from her, younger, even pretty. 'Oh, darling, don't be silly,' she said affectionately. 'Monster, indeed! He was just an ordinary man.'

FIRST FLOOR FRONT

FIRST FLOOR FRONT

I was seven when we moved to Parclease. Our house in London's east end had been destroyed during the Blitz, and after several years in 'temporary' accommodation, we had finally been rehoused on a new estate built on the edge of the old village. The new estate was to become part of a housing development, the sort of thing they were then calling 'Garden Cities', which were to usher in a new golden age of town planning. It didn't quite work out like that, as we now know. The inhabitants of the new towns could not recreate the communities which had been destroyed by the German bombs; the residents of the old villages resented the newcomers; and the hastily constructed houses deteriorated rapidly into little better than slums.

But we didn't know that at the time, and though at seven I did not understand much of the theory behind our move, I felt the optimism of the adults around me, and that made me happy. It was summer, there was no more school for six weeks, and I had all my days ahead of me to explore my new kingdom. I don't know how it was, but in those days the summers were different. Do you remember them? Day followed perfect day of hot sunshine, the sky was always deep blue, with

161

occasionally a light, refreshing breeze or a wisp of white cloud just for a relish. It never rained, and the days seemed endless. We don't have summers like that nowadays. I wonder why?

For a while I wandered about the new estate which, being far from completion, was a boy's heaven of newly-cleared sites, half-built houses, stacks of bricks and planks, and mysterious, forbidden machinery. I annoyed the building workers, took the skin off every protruding surface of my skinny body, and narrowly avoided death several times while climbing about the scaffolding. Finally, one day, feeling I had become more than usually unpopular with a certain Irish foreman of limited but emphatic vocabulary, I filched a piece of putty (without which in those days I felt almost naked) and wandered off to explore the old village.

Parclease was not suffering its first invasion. The original village, clustering around the traditional complement of church, green, pond, and smithy, had been extended in Victorian times by several streets of handsome three-storey town houses, and a new high street of shops and a carbuncular Methodist chapel had grown up to serve them. I was walking through this residential area when I was hailed by an imperious voice.

'Boy!'

I looked about me. I was standing beside one of those tall houses which has steps going up to the front door, and a half-basement below them, which we Londoners used to call 'the area'. The first floor had originally contained the main living rooms, and its windows were large and impressive, but at some time this particular house had been divided up into lodgings, and it had all the hallmarks of shabbiness and a motley collection of different curtains. At the window of what must once have been the drawing room, but was now simply First Floor Front, a woman was beckoning me.

'Boy, come here,' she called, seeing she had my attention. As I couldn't approach any closer across the area, I supposed she must want me to enter the house, and as if she had heard my thought, she nodded vigorously and said, 'That's right, the door is open. Come in, come in.'

There was nothing unusual in her request. In those days grown-ups expected children to make themselves useful, and any adult, whether related or even known to one or not, might send one on an errand. We were expected to do as we were told, and I don't know that we were the worse for it.

I went up the steps and through the open front door into the hallway, which was dark, painted brown and cream, and smelled of cabbage and boots. The stairs mounted ahead of me, and a passage ran down the side of them towards the back of the house. To my

163

left was the door to the room to which I had been summoned, an ordinary panelled door finished in that curious ginger varnish the Victorians loved, with a china doorknob and finger plate. I tapped upon it, and opened it cautiously.

The room inside was of handsome proportions, with a huge marble fireplace, decorative cornices and a ceiling rose of serpentine elaboration. It might still have been taken for a drawing room by its furnishings, for it was filled with chairs upholstered in red velvet, little tables and what-nots covered in china ornaments, parlour palms and aspidistras in brass bowls. The walls were covered with pictures, and the mantelpiece bore a velvet cover with a bobble fringe and was crammed with more ornaments, candlesticks, framed photographs and a clock.

The only dissonant features were the bed in the far corner—though a noble effort had been made to disguise it with a plush cover and a heap of cushions—and the gas ring in the hearth.

There was so much to look at in the room that I might have stood there with my mouth open for ten minutes had not my attention been demanded forcibly, even irritably, by the occupant herself. She was seated on a *chaise longue* by the window, her back very straight, her hands folded in her lap. You don't see old ladies like that anymore, and even then they were a threatened species. She wore a long black skirt—not for her the modern craze for displaying legs—and a lace blouse with long sleeves and a high neck. Round her neck she wore a number of chains and necklaces, topped off with a pearl choker, and her iron-grey hair was done up behind, with the visible area of it crimped into rigid parallel waves.

'Well, have you done staring?' she said sharply. 'Come here, boy. Stand here in front of me while I look at you.'

I approached and stood on the spot she had indicated, while she subjected me to a scrutiny at least as detailed as mine of her. I could not guess her age—to a seven-year-old, old is old, without degrees. She was thin, with a long, narrow face, bright eyes, and a small mouth which seemed very full of teeth. Only the fact that the teeth themselves were also long and thin enabled them all to fit in, and perhaps because of them, she spoke in a curious way, with her lips pursed like a mouse about to nibble a nut, clipping off her words as if biting them with those long teeth.

'You're very dirty,' was the result of her long scrutiny. I was not offended: it was a just comment.

'I've been playing on the building site,' I said.

'Hmm. Are you one of the newcomers? I suppose you are. I haven't seen you before. What is that in your hand?'

'Putty,' I told her, offering it for inspection. She eyed it like a bird, her head a little tilted. Evidently she decided it was a gift for she gave a little smile and a gracious nod, and took it from me.

'Thank you,' she said. 'Most acceptable.' I was disappointed, but considered quickly that I could always get some more; and I was rather flattered by the unaccustomed sensation of giving a present to a grown-up. 'What's your name, boy?' she asked next.

'Michael,' I replied. She nodded.

'That is quite satisfactory. Mine is Miss Stivvens. Well, now you are here, I had better entertain you. Go to that cupboard over there and bring me the tin you will find inside.'

The tin was large and round, and decorated with wonderful, highly-coloured scenes. There were strange, white, pinnacled buildings; jungles seething with tigers, snakes and monkeys; elephants in glorious caparison; bejewelled rajahs and black servants in white robes.

'You like it?' Miss Stivvens asked.

'It's beautiful,' I said sincerely. She took it from me and turned it round in her hands, smiling.

'Lovely, lovely India. I went there when I was a child no more than your age,' she said rapturously, and then interrupting herself with a sharp question, she asked, 'How old are you?'

'Seven,' I said.

'Quite right,' she replied, and resumed her reminiscences. 'I lived there for twelve years— oh, the parties! The tiger-shoots, the polo, the handsome young officers!' She was silent, and I could see from her face that she was far away, which was all very well for her. I fidgeted, and she came back to reality, and opened the tin. 'Ginger-nuts,' she said. 'Just right with Madeira. You like Madeira, of course?'

Of course, I had never tasted it, but thought it safer to assent. She poured two glasses of brown liquid and gave me one, and offered me the biscuit tin. With Madeira in one hand and a ginger-nut in the other, she proposed a toast. 'To friendship,' she proclaimed. We both drank. The Madeira was delicious, a brown, sweet, burnt taste, with a fieriness behind it that delighted me and made me choke a little.

'You like it?' she asked sharply. I nodded, coughing, and she frowned. 'It occurs to me that probably you are not supposed to drink wine. You had better not tell anyone about the Madeira. Have another ginger-nut, and I will tell you about India. That was the place to be young!'

I left some time later, my head reeling, not only with Madeira (which I now thought definitely superior to ginger beer, the strongest liquor I had ever yet tasted) but also with Miss Stivvens's tales of Lovely India where she had spent, in her own words, 'the madcap, merry days' of her youth.

When I arrived home, it was teatime, and my mother had a visitor: the vicar of St Peter's, the old church on the village green, had made a courtesy call. My mother had risen to the occasion, despite the packing cases and general confusion of only just having moved in, with tea and the best lace cloth.

I was introduced, and my mother asked me where I had been.

'In the village,' I said. 'I met a lady.'

'What lady?' my mother asked anxiously.

'Miss Stivvens,' I said. 'She gave me—ginger biscuits.' At the last moment I remembered not to mention the Madeira.

'Oh Michael, I've told you before about talking to strangers, and taking sweets from them. What did you say her name was?'

'Miss Stivvens, and it wasn't sweets, and she isn't a stranger. She lives in a big house in the village,' I defended myself, and the vicar came unexpectedly to my aid.

'Oh, you mean Miss Stevens. She's quite harmless, poor old thing. She must be nearly ninety now. Perfectly respectable, not very well off now, I'm afraid, like so many of our older residents, though she comes of a good family. They were very well-to-do when she was younger. Of course,' he added, looking down at me sternly, 'your mother is quite right about not talking to strangers as a rule, but in this

168

case,' he continued, smiling at my mother, 'I'm sure there is no harm done.'

'She's got lots of things in her house,' I offered. 'And she told me all about Lovely India, about tigers and things. She said she'd show me some photographs if I went back again. May I?'

My mother hesitated, and looked to the vicar for advice. He nodded reassuringly to her and said, 'I'm sure it would be a most Christian act. Poor Miss Stevens is all alone in the world, and doesn't get out much. I visit her when I can, but she must often feel lonely.'

'Very well, then, Michael,' my mother said, 'but don't be a nuisance, and don't stay too long and tire her out. And now you had better go and wash your hands for tea.'

*　　　*　　　*

I went back to see Miss Stivvens—for so I continued to think of her—the next day. She gave me Madeira and ginger-nuts, and showed me her photographs, dim, brown and formal, of ladies in long skirts and queer hats on verandahs with white-robed servants always in the background, of men with moustaches and military uniforms, sitting on polo ponies, or holding guns and posing with one foot on the corpse of some creature they had slain.

There was one of a lady all in black, with huge wide skirts and a funny little black lace bonnet on her head, sitting in a low-slung carriage which was harnessed to a pair of goats.

'My dear mother, in her victoria. She had it sent over from England specially, but Papa wouldn't let her have any of the ponies, so she had the syce train a pair of goats. That's the syce, Panjit, holding the goats. He taught me to ride. Dear Panjit!'

A photograph of a man with his hair parted in the middle, slicked down hard on his head and a huge curly moustache, standing with his hand on the back of an armchair and a parlour palm behind him, drew forth a deep sigh.

'That was my beloved Jeremy. He was so handsome! Such lovely moustaches, and he danced so well! We were to be married, you know. That's me, in the chair.'

I looked at the wasp-waisted creature with the bird's nest hair seated in the photograph, and found it impossible to believe. 'Why didn't you marry him?' I asked.

She sighed again, more deeply. 'Papa didn't approve, and when we went back to England, I lost touch with him, for one was not allowed to write to gentlemen in those days. Oh, lovely India, how I missed it! I was so happy there.'

She told me more stories, about boar-hunts in the mountains, and dances at the Rajah's palace. She told me the names of all her brothers, every servant and most of the polo ponies; and all the young men who had been in love with her and whom she had refused for her beloved Jeremy's sake. I listened to it all, entranced. It was a fairy-tale place to me, and my mental picture of Lovely India was a combination of the biscuit tin and the room I sat in, as vivid as it was unreal.

When I finally left, trotting down the steps in the bright sunshine, my head stuffed with snakes, syces, elephants and white kid gloves, a flash of colour caught my attention, and I looked down to see bright blue curtains at the barred basement window in the area, which I had never noticed before.

Standing between them, beckoning to me, was another old lady, her mouth making the inevitable shape of 'Boy!' I hesitated, glancing back at the front door, and she shook her head, gesturing firmly that I was to come down the area steps and enter through the separate basement door.

My experience with Miss Stivvens had proved interesting, and so I obeyed willingly, entering through the basement door into the passage of what had once been the kitchen regions. There was a smell of damp which was unpleasant, and after the hot sunshine outside, the air struck very cold; but when I pushed open the door to my left which led into the room directly under Miss Stivvens's, I found myself at once in a very different atmosphere.

The room was warm and smelled of baking. It was simply furnished, with a floral print

171

wallpaper, a sofa and two armchairs covered in chintz, and in the middle of the room a scrubbed wooden kitchen table with four wooden chairs around it. On it was a baking-rack on which a new batch of cakes steamed gently. In the great arch of the fireplace was an old-fashioned cooking range, and through the bars of the firebox I could see the flames of a good blaze. It struck me as odd that there should be a fire lit in the middle of a very hot summer, but certainly the room was not too warm.

As if she had heard my thought, the room's occupant said, 'These basements are so damp, you need a fire all year round. Well, Michael, don't just stand at the door. Come in.'

She was as round as Miss Stivvens was spare, a plump body straining at the seams of a black satin dress, a round face with round eyes, and white hair done up on top of her head in a great, round bun. She smiled at me cheerfully, displaying a set of false teeth that seemed to have been made for someone else, so badly did they fit. I was fascinated by them, for when she spoke they seemed imbued with a life of their own, sliding about in her mouth so that I had to concentrate to understand what she was saying. Perhaps because of my preoccupation, it did not strike mc as odd that she knew my name. There was nothing else particularly odd about her, except that she was very pale, as if living in the basement away from the sunlight had bleached her.

I thought momentarily of the sort of fungus that grows in the dark, but quickly thrust the image away as she said, 'I expect you'd like some tea, wouldn't you? I've made some cakes—they've got currants in them. I hope you like currants?' I nodded, and she bustled off to the range where the kettle was just beginning to boil, and set about making the tea.

'I expect you'd like it strong, wouldn't you? I know grown-ups will never let children have their tea strong. They say it's bad for them and silly things like that, but milky tea is so horrid, isn't it? Do sit down, and help yourself to a cake. I always think they taste better when they're still warm, but I was never allowed to eat them until they got cold when I was a girl. Such a waste, I thought.'

I did as I was told, sat down at the table, and took a cake. It was delicious, and I concurred fervently with her notions on cake-eating. The room was pleasant and comfortable, quite different from Miss Stivvens' kingdom above. The old lady came back to the table bearing a teapot the like of which I had never seen before: it was in the shape of a thatched cottage, complete with doors and windows, and even had hollyhocks growing up the walls. The thatched roof was the lid, and it had a handle and spout growing out of its ends like ears.

173

She noticed me admiring it, and said, 'Do you like it? It was always one of my favourites. I had lots of lovely things, but bit by bit I had to sell them, and then I lost so many things in the war. I had a cream-jug in the shape of a cow once, but I don't know what became of that.'

She looked vaguely around the room as if expecting to see it, and then returned her gaze to me. 'I'm Miss Mumbleberry, by the way. I've seen you before, on your way to visit *her*. You do visit Her, don't you?'

'Miss Stivvens?' I said without thinking, and she laughed.

'Is that what you call her? Oh yes, that's very good! That pretentious way she talks, all prunes and prisms, as if she was too good for the rest of us. Miss Stivvens! Yes, I like that.'

I wasn't sure what pretentious meant, but I gathered that the laughter was derisive, and felt embarrassed. After all, I had just been partaking of Miss Stivvens's hospitality, and it didn't seem right to laugh at her.

Miss Mumbleberry seemed to understand my dilemma. 'Are you her friend?' she asked, and when I hesitated, she said, 'Come, speak up, don't be shy. Tell the truth and shame the Devil. Are you her friend, or aren't you?'

'I think so,' I said. She nodded.

'Fair enough,' she said. 'I was her friend once. Not any more! Not after what she did.'

'What did she do?'

'I can't speak of it,' she said, closing her eyes and turning her face upwards to heaven. 'Too dreadful!' She opened her eyes abruptly. 'She betrayed me, you know. It was during the war. Before that, she and I were—like that.' She did not demonstrate what 'that' was, but nodded significantly at me, as though I ought to know. 'But afterwards, we never spoke to each other again. So much for friendship!' she finished triumphantly, and pushed the cakes towards me again.

'Did you go to Lovely India with her?' I asked with interest.

She looked contemptuous. 'India! I did not! I spent my girlhood here in England, and I don't think better of those who went running off abroad to live with a lot of black people, even if they did have servants at their beck and call. Not,' she added severely as if I had argued, 'that I didn't have servants. When I was a girl, at Beadings—that was the name of the house, you know—dear, dear Beadings! I shall never forget it.'

'Did you have parties, too?' I asked, and she smiled, giving the full benefit of her china teeth.

'Oh, such parties! And dances! During the hunting season we had dances every week, and when the men came down to shoot, dear, dear Beadings was full of guests every Saturday to Monday. You can't imagine! And my coming-out ball—I was presented, of course.' She nodded to me, as I nodded back, having little idea what she was talking about, but happy enough to listen and watch those amazing teeth. Dear, dear Beadings, to my bemused mind, became a kind of English-pastoral version of Lovely India, denuded of tigers and elephants, but teeming instead with grouse, pheasants, foxes and hares; and if the servants were not black, they were at least plentiful, and dressed instead in something called livery, which in my bemusement I imagined as dark brown and very shiny.

When I had eaten as much tea as I could, I took my leave.

'Come and see me whenever you like,' Miss Mumbleberry said. 'I'm sure you'll be better off here than with *her*, with her Madeira and her nonsense. Filling a boy's head with pig-sticking and such heathen ideas! You come and see me, boy, and never mind *her*, with her First Floor Front airs.'

*   *   *

Though feeling rather important as the object of such rivalry, I did not mention Miss Mumbleberry at home, thinking that perhaps two strange old ladies might be rather gilding the lily. When I next visited Miss Stivvens, however, I was determined to find out why they had quarrelled, and mentioned straightaway that I had had tea with Miss

Mumbleberry. Miss Stivvens's reaction was to laugh as derisively as had her former friend.

'Mumbleberry! That's a good name for her. Mumble she does, with those dreadful, vulgar teeth, which never fitted her properly, even when she first had them. Mumbleberry indeed!'

'Isn't that her name, then?'

'Not quite. It's Mundlebury; but yours will do just as well!'

'She said you used to be friends,' I offered. Miss Stivvens looked grim.

'Did she, indeed! Well, that's true enough. I was her friend, and look how she paid me out! I don't care for treachery. I expect my friends to be loyal to me. Remember that, Michael.'

'But what did you do?' I asked. 'She said you betrayed her. In the war, and that made her stop being your friend.'

Miss Stivvens grew red with indignation 'How dare she! It was she who betrayed our friendship! After all I'd done for her, too! It was disloyal, and I can't forgive that. The impudence, to blame it on to me!'

'But what did she do?' I asked, but she shook her head.

'The worst thing one friend could do to another,' was all she would tell me. 'And I don't know that I like you visiting her, Michael. I think I should forbid it.' She looked at me thoughtfully, and I looked back, a touch defiantly; but after a while she said, 'On

177

second thoughts, I suppose there is no harm in it. You will be able to tell me what she is up to. You must keep an eye on her for me, and tell me what she says to you. You will be my representative in her camp, my spy, if you like. But don't forget, boy, that you are my friend, first and foremost.'

*   *   *

So that long, lovely summer passed, my first summer in Parclease, and the one I remember best in all my childhood. Day after day I explored my new surroundings. I discovered the joys of the countryside which I had never known before, town boy that I was; and when I was tired of lanes, fields and hedges, of catching guppies in the stream, of helping the haymakers, of climbing trees, of making plantain guns and grass-blade whistles, of stealing apples and trespassing in private woods, I would make my way, hot and dusty and usually very dirty, to the big Victorian house, and visit Miss Stivvens and Miss Mumbleberry.

Half-dazed by the long day of sunshine and new experiences, my skin smelling like hot biscuits, and prickling from the hay which somehow always got down inside my shirt, I would sit in a velvet chair with a glass of Madeira, or lean my elbows on a scrubbed table and drink strong tea, and listen while they span their stories for me. Miss Stivvens told me about Lovely India and the last days of the Raj, and Miss Mumbleberry told me about Dear, Dear Beadings, and a world almost as remote to me then, the great era of the English Country House.

Miss Stivvens showed me photographs, and brought out from a trunk under her bed remnants of her old glory, dresses and shawls, fans, gloves and feathers, which were as strange and exotic as theatrical costumes. Sometimes she would dress up for me, and once she put records on an old wind-up gramophone, strange scratchy songs and quavering voices, and we danced solemnly upon her Turkish carpet, her eyes bright with the memories of beloved Jeremy and his beautiful moustache.

Miss Mumbleberry had no photographs and no music, but one by one she got out her treasures to show to me: pieces of old china painted in lovely bright colours, unlike anything we had at home; a picture of a lady in a crinoline dress made entirely of feathers, and a mirror whose frame was made of tiny seashells stuck onto wood in patterns; another teapot in the shape of a cat with one paw lifted for the spout; a little cedarwood box which played a tiny tinkling tune when the lid was lifted. The odd thing was that I never saw any of these things lying about the room, either before or afterwards. She seemed to produce

179

them out of thin air to attract my attention, and the next time I came, they would have disappeared again.

They were terrible rivals, and I could never find out any more about what had caused the breach between them, other than that it was something Miss S thought Miss M had done, and conversely, something Miss M thought Miss S had failed to do. They were united in regarding the breach as irreversible, owing to the other's treachery. But despite vowing never to speak to each other again, they remained burningly curious about each other's lives, and I was called upon to describe in minute detail every inch of each room, every article in it, and every word the other had spoken to me. Their hunger for knowledge of each other was so great that once or twice I suggested tentatively that they might visit, but the suggestion was dismissed instantly— fiercely by Miss Mumbleberry and perhaps a touch wistfully by Miss Stivvens.

As the days went by, I began to feel that I liked Miss Stivvens more than Miss Mumbleberry. It was true that the latter gave me delicious cakes, and flattered me overtly, saying how much she enjoyed my visits; but I preferred Miss Stivvens's detachment, and her belongings were more interesting, and her stories infinitely more exciting. I learned a great deal about Lovely India, and developed a taste for Madeira that has never left me to this day. While I went to see Miss Stivvens because I wanted to, my visits to Miss Mumbleberry became more of a duty than a pleasure, and were continued at least partly on Miss Stivvens's insistence.

There was something I did not quite like about Miss Mumbleberry. The smell of damp and mould in the basement would sometimes penetrate into her room from the passage outside, and the white softness of her face still reminded me of fungus. I didn't like the way she fixed her eyes on my face when she spoke to me—Miss Stivvens's eyes were more usually fixed on the distant past—or the overt way she tried to subvert me from her rival: Miss Stivvens at least feigned indifference to my preferences. And despite the hot summer outside, and the fire invariably burning in the grate, the basement was sometimes unwelcomingly cold.

I think it must have been the awareness that she was not my favourite which led Miss Mumbleberry to give me a present. I went in to tea one day, and there was a magnificent chocolate cake on the table (and in those days of shortages and the hangover of rationing, a chocolate cake was still a rarity). When we had drunk our tea and I had eaten two large slices of it, Miss Mumbleberry brought her hands up out of her lap, cupped to conceal something held within them.

'I've got something for you, Michael,' she

said, fixing her eyes hungrily on my face. 'A little present for you, to say thank you for making an old lady very happy. I really look forward to your visits, you know. I should be very sorry if they stopped. So I've got this little present for you.'

She placed it on the table in front of me. I expect all of you have seen something like it— they became quite commonplace in later years—but at that time it was something quite unusual, and I had never seen anything like it. It was one of those glass domes showing a little winter scene. The dome was filled with water containing tiny scraps of some white substance, so that when you shook it, the little white scraps swirled up and fell slowly like snow. The tiny scene was like something from a theatre: a turreted castle, a few fir trees, a frozen pond, and two skaters. They were Victorian ladies in long, full skirts, short capes, and little black skating boots, with pink painted faces framed by little bonnets. Each skated upon one foot, the other sticking out behind, with their hands out for balance. They were at opposite ends of the pond, facing each other, but frozen apart at that fixed distance forever, while the snow fell softly, inexorably, covering them.

I was entranced by it. I shook it, and watched until all the snow had settled, and then shook it again. When I looked up I encountered Miss Mumbleberry's hungry gaze, and said, 'Is it really for me?'

'Yes, really,' she said, looking pleased. 'I had it in my own room at dear, dear Beadings, when I was a little girl no more than your age. I was always very fond of it, so I thought you might like to have it.'

'Thank you very much,' I said fervently, feeling ashamed that I had not liked her. 'I think it's lovely.'

'You must keep it in your room at home. And when you look at it, you must always remember me. You will, won't you, Michael? You will remember me?'

'Yes, I will,' I promised uneasily, and she seemed satisfied.

'Have another piece of chocolate cake,' she said.

*   *   *

The day came when I arrived at the house to find that, for the first time that summer, the front door was closed. The curtains of the First Floor Front room were drawn, too, which worried me. When I went and knocked on the door, there was no answer. Could Miss Stivvens have gone away? I wondered. And yet, surely she would have mentioned it when I last saw her, the day before yesterday. I had not been able to see her yesterday, because my mother had taken me into the town to buy my new school uniform. I would be starting next week at my first Big School, and had lots to tell my friend.

I decided to go downstairs and ask Miss Mumbleberry whether she knew where Miss Stivvens had gone, and I was halfway down the area steps before I noticed that there were no curtains at her window at all. I knocked on the door, receiving no reply, though I had half expected that, and then went to the window.

By pressing my face against the bars, I was able to look in. The basement room was quite empty—not just of Miss Mumbleberry, you understand, but of furniture, too. There was the fireplace and the kitchen range, though there was no fire, but the floorboards were bare, and there was nothing else in the room at all. She's moved, I thought; but there was something that was worrying me about that room, and it was a moment before I realised what it was.

The wallpaper was different. Instead of the little floral pattern I had grown so used to over the weeks, there were large blue cabbage-roses from floor to ceiling. Now a person moving house doesn't take their wallpaper with them, I knew that. I was upset and worried. I ran up the area steps, and stood in the afternoon sunshine wondering what to do. The church clock, out of sight but not out of earshot, struck the half hour, and I had a happy thought: the vicar had said that he visited Miss Stivvens. Perhaps he would know where she was.

His housekeeper opened the vicarage door to me, and frowned down at me as housekeepers automatically did at small boys.

'Now then, what do you want?' she asked discouragingly.

'Can I see the vicar?' I asked. She didn't look as though it were likely, so I added, 'It's important, really it is.'

'What's your name?' she asked. I told her, and she bid me wait where I was, went inside and shut the door. A few minutes later she opened it again, told me I could come in, commanding me fiercely to wipe my feet. The vicar received me in his study. He stood up when I came in, and came to put a hand on my shoulder, giving me a grave but kindly look.

'I can guess what you've come about,' he said, and my heart sank. 'Is it Miss Stevens?'

I nodded. 'I just went to her house, but the curtains are drawn, and when I knocked there was no answer.'

'I'm afraid, my boy, that I have sad news for you. Miss Stevens died on Tuesday night.'

I had half expected the words, but they struck me dumb. I had no experience of death; I did not know how to think about it. The vicar went on speaking.

'She died quite quietly in her own bed, you know, and there's nothing really to be sorry about on her behalf. She'd had a long and full life, and she has now gone to join our

Heavenly Father in eternal bliss, so although we shall miss her, we should really be glad for her, shouldn't we?'

I nodded, because that seemed to be the required answer.

'I can tell you that your visits did a great deal to brighten the last days of her life. It was a kind and Christian thing you did, my boy, something you can be proud to remember. She spoke of you to me on several occasions, you know, Michael, and do you know what she called you?' I shook my head. 'She called you "her friend". Isn't that something to remember with pride?'

I looked up at him. 'But what about Miss Mumbleberry?' I asked. He looked puzzled. 'Her friend—at least, they used to be friends, but they quarrelled about something.'

'Oh, you mean Miss Mundlebury? Yes, I have heard Miss Stevens talk about her. They lived together for many years and were the closest of friends, quite inseparable. Miss Stevens told you about her too, did she?'

'Yes,' I said. 'And she lived in the basement.'

'In the basement? Of course she didn't. What made you think she did?'

I could not answer that. I felt confused. 'But what happened to her? Where did she go?'

'Miss Mundlebury? Oh, that was a very sad thing, Michael. The two ladies were caught up in a bomb blast, during an air raid. They were pulled out from the rubble, but poor Miss

186

Mundlebury was dead, though Miss Stevens escaped with hardly a scratch. Miss Stevens was quite inconsolable, I gather.' He paused, and went on, 'Miss Stevens had a curious way of talking about it—as if Miss Mundlebury had somehow betrayed her by being killed. She called it treachery and said she could not forgive her. Such an odd thing! But of course, she was very old, and the old have their fancies.'

'Yes,' I said, my mind reeling. 'But, sir, who did live in the basement, then?'

'Well, it's been empty since March, when the Muntings left. Such a nice couple—they've got a council house at last, and not before time with the baby on the way. They had been there for nearly four years, waiting for their house, and before that, there was a Mr Arnold, as I remember.'

I could make no sense of all this. I grasped again, like a drowning man, for reality.

'But, please, sir, when did Miss Mumbleberry die?'

The vicar frowned in thought. 'I really don't know, my boy. It was before I came to Parclease. I don't know if Miss Stevens ever mentioned the date, but it was very many years ago, certainly.'

'But you said it was an air raid,' I said desperately. 'And she said it was during the war—'

The vicar's brow cleared. 'The first war, my

boy, the First World War. I'm afraid there are lots of old people who still think of it as the only one.'

*   *   *

I still have my snow-scene. It sits on my bedside table, and I often pick it up, shake it, and watch the snow fall on the castle, the pond and the skaters: the two ladies skating towards each other, arms outstretched. Yes, I'm sure of it, for now I look more closely, I can see that the pink, painted faces are smiling. I think I understand now. I was a go-between, whose purpose was to satisfy the hunger for communication that not even the burning anger and disappointment of thirty years could blunt.

I keep my promise, at least in part: I do think about Miss Mumbleberry when I look at it. But I think about Miss Stivvens too, and hope that, once they were together again on the same side of death, they were able to forgive each other for having been parted, and be friends again. Perhaps I brought the reconciliation closer? I don't know whether I hope so, or fear so.

THE CAKES OF WRATH

THE CAKES OF WRATH

'She lived,' says Mrs Carnwath in a tone of disapproval which just fails to mask the wistfulness of envy, 'a life of unexampled idleness. She grew as fat as a boa-constrictor. Well, you can imagine!'

'Imagine,' agrees Miss Widdrington sadly from the other side of the table, subduing the intellectual in favour of the economic judgement. Besides, she is a meek little soul and has great difficulty with the concept that she may occasionally be right and others wrong.

The tea-room upstairs at Fullers in Princes Street is filled, as always at this time of day, with the respectable ladies of Edinburgh, predominantly spinsters, but with a sprinkling of widows—easy to distinguish by their fur coats, their air of opulence, their faintly patronising attitude towards their unmarried sisters.

The tea-room is a comfortable, comforting place. The tablecloths are always starched and white, though a close examination might discover a neat, almost invisible darn here and there, which might have been worked by a fairy's fingers, so tiny are the white silk stitches. The silver, though elderly and worn thin, is always brightly polished. The tea is always hot and strong, and the walnut layer cake is famed throughout the civilised world, and in Glasgow.

But more, the tea-room recreates for the ladies the vanished world of their childhood. The dark panelling and the red Turkey carpet have overtones of Papa's study; evocative as the tinkling ritual of afternoon tea, the fragrance of mothballs, starch and lavender polish. The maitre d'hotel is the father they would have liked to have and sometimes, falsely, remember—remote, stern, and yet with a twinkle in the eye suggesting a delicious vein of sympathy just under the surface, ready to be mined.

And the waitresses are the housemaids of their childhood: ageless—or rather youthless— in black dresses and white aprons, string-coloured hair limp under white caps, they creak from table to table on shapeless, martyred feet. In the winter their noses drip dismally, in the summer their ankles swell, and at all seasons the faulty hoses of their veins strain visibly against the dung-coloured lisle of their stockings. Like the housemaids of yore they are featureless, interchangeable, and yet impossible to ignore. A brooding presence of tepid resentment attaches to each pair of scrubbed, red hands bringing the plates of scones and trays of tea; a mute but palpable criticism lurks abrasively behind the flat eyes and tortured accents; and conversation burns up the brighter for it, and laughter grows more theatrical at their arrival with the fresh hot water and the clean butter knife.

'She lived,' says Mrs Carnwath, 'in that big house on the corner of Strathfillan Gardens.' She is an oddly-shaped monument in purple, with the unevenness of a large woman grown small. Her neck and arms are thin, but her bosom is extensive, and upon its shelf, as upon a jeweller's velvets, she displays rows and rows of pearls, as if at some time she has decided that since there is no possibility of concealing it, it might as well be made useful. It is the only way in which it has ever been useful, for Mrs Carnwath is, and always intended to be, childless. Thus Nature mocks her own creations, saving the best practical jokes for those who can least appreciate them.

Mrs Carnwath's face is chalky pink, and has the collapsed, unreliable look of an insufficiently inflated balloon. Her hair, which turned unexpectedly yellow after the death of her husband, seems to grow in several of the wrong directions, owing to the weekly attentions of the little coiffeuse in the salon on the corner of Hanover Street. It pulls the skin of her temples tight, giving her a look of surprise as far down as the eyes; below, she has disappointed lines, and a mouth which quivers with well-bred disapproval. She would find no human folly particularly surprising.

'It's much too large for one person. She

must quite rattle in it. Such a crime, when one thinks—'

'When one thinks,' echoes Miss Widdrington obediently, nodding away across the table like the obliging creature she has always been. Outside the sun shines on Princes Street Gardens; and on the Castle Rock, stranded above the city like a great, black whale, black and shiny as anthracite; and on the honey-coloured castle above it, which, faintly disreputable as beauty must always appear amidst austerity, drifts amongst the clouds like an actress swathed in gauzy scarves, seems to move amongst them, like Isadora Duncan. The soot of the city has blackened every other edifice, but cannot rise as high as the castle; tumbles through the damp air to coat the humbler dwellings below, leaving the castle aloof and palely loitering.

Once, long ago when the world was young, Miss Widdrington walked the length of Princes Street Gardens without once taking her eyes from the castle battlements; gazing, as she could not gaze upon the face of her lover Hugh, instead upon the walls which concealed him. As love directed her eyes, so it lightened her tread, and she glided from step to unseen step and never once stumbled.

Yet only last year Miss Widdrington's mother, walking along the same paths, tripped and fell, despite having both her eyes and all her attention at her disposal. Miss

194

Widdrington's mother was not young and not in love, and the ground, it must be supposed, resented her. At all events, stumble she did over some minor irregularity, and broke her hip—a severe enough penalty, one might have thought, for outliving passion.

Miss Widdrington does not now gaze at the bright scene to her left beyond the window, nor is her memory thronged with the young man she loved and his many companions, who fell in the fields of Flanders, the better to demonstrate that human flesh, even when young and passionate, does not readily withstand the impact of small, metal objects moving at high velocity—a point of fact on which mankind seems curiously hard to satisfy. Miss Widdrington has, for the moment, forgotten Hugh as completely as he has forgotten her.

She is looking at her plate, for she has ordered a poached egg on toast, and she loves poached eggs. Her mind is bright with a thousand poached eggs of the past; they gleam like daisies against the dark sward of memory. Each is perfect, the very paradigm of poached-eggness: the white firm and virginal, the golden centre yielding its warm, sensual richness to the importunity of a corner of toast speared upon the fork.

Yet though her egg has had a thousand predecessors, she loves this egg sincerely. Miss Widdrington does not make the mistake of so many of her sex, of believing that love must remain historically singular to be genuine.

But even as blameless a love as this—and so secure, one would have thought, of consummation—brings its pains. Miss Widdrington, though she nods and echoes, is not really attending to Mrs Carnwath's words. She gazes upon her egg, and hesitates in an agony of doubt and growing frustration. It is no failure of love which troubles her thoughts, but a problem of etiquette: if she were at home, Miss Widdrington would dip the corner of her toast in the egg-yolk, as she always does; but can she—dare she—do so here? Will not Mrs Carnwath think her common?

A dread of disapproval has always governed Miss Widdrington's actions, even her very thoughts. She has tried all her life to please those about her, to live up to the standards with which she has invested them in her mind. Now doubt gives way to disappointment. She must not risk a solecism. Sadness lays its familiar hand across her heart, and she cuts a segment of egg-white of similar proportion to the toast-corner, lays the former upon the latter, and transfers them demurely to her mouth.

Thus it was, too, when Hugh's mother came to show Miss Widdrington's mother the War Office telegram announcing his death. Monumental in black, like a draped piano— expansive, almost festive in the accoutrements of her permitted, maternal grief, like a civic building hung with bunting for Remembrance Sunday—Mrs McGill bent a pitying smile upon Mrs Widdrington and said, 'Of course, there is no need for your girl to mourn my Hugh. There was no formal engagement, after all.'

And Miss Widdrington obediently folded in her lap the hands which would have rent her hair, cancelled frenzy, and raised her voice not in a howl like King Lear, but to ask if Mrs McGill would take more tea.

Mrs McGill was thus able to keep her mourning exclusive, and it broke out all over her in a violent rash of disfiguring black scarves, feathers, and Whitby jet ornaments, which defied all treatment and remained with her until death. Mrs McGill took tea at Fullers every afternoon, and had a special table reserved for her in the corner by the window, as befitted her tragic stature. She never spoke to Miss Widdrington, even when she was seated at the next table, as though she feared that notice might encourage Miss Widdrington to develop similar symptoms.

'She has a mahogany tea-caddy, with a little lock on it, and a key. She keeps it locked, though she no more has a parlour-maid than I have,' continues Mrs Carnwath, breathless with muted outrage. 'But what can you expect of a woman who uses a silver chafing-dish for flower arrangements?' she adds scornfully.

197

'Imelda! It's not what I'd call a Christian name.'

'Not a *Christian* name,' Miss Widdrington agrees carefully. The white of the egg and the surrounding toast all eaten away, she has only the yolk left now, intact upon its own self-shaped little raft, and she hesitates on the brink of consummation, delaying the moment deliciously—as, when a child, she would wake on Christmas morning and turn her head away from the fireplace before opening her eyes, so that she should not at once see the miraculously-filled stocking she knew would be hanging there. Anticipation is a sweet and solitary sin, and peculiarly human; though perhaps the lion, as it pauses a moment and thoughtfully licks the hide of the wildebeest it has just slain, knows something of it.

'A cook-general is all she ever had, for all that she was a Frobisher, or so she claims,' says Mrs Carnwath. 'But the silver *bonbonnière* on the sideboard, which I happen to know was a gift from Archie for her parents' twenty-fifth, is only engraved 'With love to Dick and Dolly', which is not what I'd call a testimonial.'

'No indeed,' murmurs Miss Widdrington, knife and fork poised blissfully to break open the taut capsule she has preserved until this moment.

A waitress appears at the table, stares pointedly, and walks away. Mrs Carnwath's attention is drawn to the state of her companion's plate; her own is long empty, for to Mrs Carnwath a poached egg is nothing more than a means to sustenance.

'Are you not finished, Euphemia?' she asks, and though she may believe within herself that this is a simple enquiry, what purpose can it have but to flurry Miss Widdrington, to imply a criticism of her? Can Miss Widdrington differ from Mrs Carnwath in any way that reflects to her credit? And can Miss Widdrington, with all eyes upon her, or at least the pair that signify, delay the consumption of the last of her egg any further? Of course she cannot. Two spots of red decorate her cheeks, a blush not of justifiable vexation, but of embarrassment at having thus drawn attention to her delinquency, and with a murmured apology she cuts the yolk-and-toast in two and disposes of them without pleasure in two swift gulps.

'There was no need to hurry,' Mrs Carnwath now says, the further to punish her friend, for the waitress has moved away too far to be recalled, and is attending some ladies at the far end. 'You'll give yourself indigestion if you eat so quickly.'

'I'm sorry, Janet,' says Miss Widdrington, and so she is, poor gentle soul. The best moment of her egg is wasted, and she has called down Mrs Carnwath's disapproval on her head: what more cause for sorrow could she want?

'You were saying?' Miss Widdrington

prompts, a bold move, meant to divert Mrs Carnwath's attention. 'About Archie, was it?'

Mrs Carnwath is appeased. 'Now *his* wife never wanted for anything,' she says graciously, 'for all that they lived practically in Corstorphine. But then, her father was a clergyman—Anglican, of course. You'd never see a fish-knife on her dining table!'

'Never!' sighs Miss Widdrington in agreement, the moment of anguish past. She waits for the waitress to come and clear, and is aware of an increased tension in Mrs Carnwath's bearing.

In this, Mrs Carnwath is not alone. All around the tea-room, the ladies are coming to the end of the first stage of their daily ritual. The poached eggs, the sardines, the toast, the bread-and-butter have been eaten, knives and forks have been laid down, and the conversation has welled up.

Ladies now gaze at each other across the table with deep and flattering attention, their eyes fixed upon each others' faces, their expressions wrapt as though the words dropping from their companions' lips were ravishingly important. Now every lady is a brilliant raconteuse, if she wishes. Whatever she says will be received with intense delight, any little pleasantry greeted with generous mirth: for every lady wishes to convince that this is what she has come for, this social intercourse, this stimulating converse with one's dearest friends.

Every lady wishes to make it clear that if she eats at all, it is only to secure herself a table and a measure of time to be with her friends. Every lady wishes to demonstrate by her eagerness for conversation that she has finished her tea, that she is replete, that she wishes for nothing further in the edible way.

How can it be, then, that the trolley, which a senior waitress with more than usually knotted legs has wheeled out from the kitchen region, causes each body it passes to quiver as though it were wreathed in a magnetic field? How can it be that though no lady ever looks in its direction, each knows exactly whereabouts in the room it is, and what is on it?

It is the cake-trolley of which we speak.

A tension of anxiety is building up like a head of steam. Who will be the first to beckon to the waitress? To do so is to lay oneself open to the tacit charge of gluttony, to call upon oneself the lowered eyelids of scorn, the faint and patronising smile of contempt; and yet whoever speaks first has the pick of everything on the trolley, and experience whispers to each leashed and straining appetite that the best confections will be snapped up quickly. The last-comers will have to comfort themselves over their plain cake with the knowledge of their spiritual superiority, and they are welcome to it. Cold comfort it will be, if there has been Black Forest Gateau and they have missed it.

The waitress pushes the trolley past slowly with its freight of delight: the whipped cream, the toasted nuts, the brandied fruits, the cherries, the chocolate and mocha and orange and praline; each airy castle of confection disposed beguilingly upon the snowflake of a doyley. Oh, the shattering of choux pastry, the yielding of sponge; oh, the sweet and yet somehow deliciously, obscenely mammarian flatness of cream upon the tongue!

The very words are a litany of sin. The word 'cake'—how it clots the throat and clings to the tongue! And 'pastries'—that unexpected, exotic, un-English plural! And 'gâteau', with its hint of French wickedness! How to say 'cream', how to say 'chocolate', without the voice sounding sticky with desire?

But we anticipate: first to decide how to beckon the waitress at all. The room seethes, like a mob held back by the linked arms of policemen. When the first person breaks through, all restraint will shatter.

It must be a widow, of course, who speaks. No spinster would dare to do so, for even if she is possessed of a fur coat—and abandoned enough to wear it—bearing only her father's surname she has insufficient social status to survive the calumny that would follow. Even Miss Cavendish, the Provost's daughter, who is over sixty and frightfully rich and has a real, genuine lady's maid, would not do such a thing. Miss Widdrington, of course, never even considers it. Her eyes are fixed upon Mrs Carnwath: it is she who must lead. Until she suggests calling for the trolley, Miss Widdrington must remain dumb upon the subject of confectionery.

Mrs Carnwath is seated by the aisle along which the trolley has passed, and though her faded gooseberry eyes have never appeared to stray from dear Euphemia's face, she has observed minutely in the seconds at her disposal what is upon the top, the favoured, level of the vehicle. Pillowy clouds of whipped cream scattered with toasted almonds and flaked chocolate have yielded their secrets to her sharp and sidelong look.

On the lower level there are plates of Madeira, Dundee, Battenburg, Jamaica; she has not seen them, and does not need to. They are always there. She has no interest in such geographical cakes. It is the pavlova she wants: the meringue whose airy lightness commemorates that of the *prima ballerina assoluta* of all time. There are but two, each reposing in its own paper case, frilled like a dancer's tutu, and supporting, upon a Comfituremberg of whipped cream, morsels of fresh fruit amongst which Mrs Carnwath has seen an indisputable whole strawberry.

If one of the pavlovas is to be hers, Mrs Carnwath must speak soon. She opens her mouth to make the usual, casual enquiry; but at that moment she notices the gleam in Miss Widdrington's eye. A gleam of appetite she would understand and even welcome; but is there—can it be?—something of the satirical in the look which meek little Miss Widdrington bends upon the dowager who has been so good as to befriend her?

There have been times in the past, let it be said, when Mrs Carnwath has entertained doubts of Miss Widdrington, who though she has always led a life of humility and service has occasionally, just occasionally, voiced an opinion of her own which did not coincide with received social usage. These aberrations have been infrequent and always instantly recanted, (and usually also very much regretted by Miss Widdrington), but they have left in Mrs Carnwath the faint apprehension that there lurks some little spirit of rebellion in Miss Widdrington. It is a quality of incalculability which makes Miss Widdrington dangerous to know.

And so Mrs Carnwath hesitates, and at that moment Mrs Jennings-Crowe calls for the trolley, and there is a faint hissing of released tension all around the room as if steam is escaping from an urn.

The cream cake moment has arrived.

A glow of fulfilment passes from face to face as eyes turn, now licensed, towards the object of their desire, and the murmured question is patted back and forth with all the innocence of a kitten playing with a spider.

—Will you have a cake, Hetty?

—Och, I don't know. I'm not one for the sweet things, really. Are you having one?

—I thought I might.

—Well, as long as you're having one, I might as well. Oh, waitress!

In the Carnwath-Widdrington camp the words have not yet been spoken. Mrs Carnwath continues with her normal conversation.

'It's obvious to anyone with half an eye that she's living above her means. She goes to Fraser's for her groceries, and buys tinned ham—even on weekdays! But the nice young man from Hornig's tells me she's not unknown on their premises for a purchase of white pudding, if you'll believe me!'

But her heart is not in it. There is an unusual atmosphere of tension, hesitation, and doubt at the table, and Mrs Carnwath is quite right to be suspicious, for though Miss Widdrington does not yet understand her own heart, she is nursing a small spark of resentment which, like other such small sparks, contains sufficient combustible potential to burn down Troy. Disappointed love, as usual, is at the bottom of it. Agamemnon and Achilles together were not more driven by passion thwarted and love turned sour.

Mrs Carnwath is growing desperate. Mrs

Anderson has called for the trolley now, and Mrs Anderson is also fond of the ballet. She must speak or lose the moment.

'Well, Euphemia, shall I call for the waitress? Are you for a cake?'

There, the question is out, and Mrs Carnwath waits in a state of unaccustomed anxiety for the answer. Miss Widdrington's meek and cervine gaze meets hers across the table and behind the meekness is a glow of dull resentment. Miss Widdrington herself only now becomes aware of it. As the beaten slave, who has received undeserved blows all his life without complaint, may inexplicably find one more blow is one too many, and rise up and slay his master, so now Miss Widdrington remembers the lost joy of her beloved poached egg, and wants revenge.

Mrs Carnwath spoiled Miss Widdrington's egg moment, and now at the cream cake moment has placed herself in Miss Widdrington's power. A savage joy burns in Miss Widdrington's breast, and she savours it, delaying her answer beyond the point where Mrs Carnwath can believe she will answer unprompted.

Oh foolish Mrs Carnwath! Leaning forward a little, and betraying, by a quiver in her voice, the urgency of her interest in the matter, she repeats the question.

'Euphemia! Shall you have a cake?'

Miss Widdrington's smile is as red and

glittering and mirthless as the tiger's, as she takes her revenge for all the disappointments of her meek and serviceable life.

'No thank you, Janet. I don't think I will.'

MISSING

MISSING

As she turned into Ealing Broadway Miss Mandeville glanced sideways, as she always did, at her reflection in the plate glass window of the draper's shop on the corner.

She wished she could break herself of the habit. It wasn't even as though it were the sin of vanity, which might at least have been enjoyable, for she knew that what she saw would not please her: a tall, thin, bony woman in a good if dull, tweed suit and sensible, handmade shoes. Mother believed in 'Buying the Best' and 'the Folly of False Economy', which meant that Miss Mandeville rarely had the pleasure of throwing anything away, or of shopping for anything new. Their clothes and shoes and the furnishings of The Laurels, right down to the bath towels and dish-cloths, would last for ever.

Face neither pretty nor ugly, merely mild, with foolish, nervous eyes, rather like a horse or a heifer, she always thought—not that that ought to be a disparagement, for she had always considered horses and cows delightful creatures, but there it was.

Hair grey now—oh the sorrow of glories past!—and cut in a more moderate version of the Eton crop she had assumed long ago to annoy Mother. A pretty good notion, she had thought at the time, for after all, the hair was indisputably hers, and nothing, not even Mother's rage, could restore what was cut off. But Mother, with all the strategic skill learned over years of skirmishes, had turned defeat into victory by claiming to like it.

'It quite suits you,' she had said, 'and after all, you're twenty-one now, so you can do as you like. You ought to start to take an interest in your appearance, or you'll never find a husband, and then who'll look after you when I'm gone? I won't live for ever, you know.'

Mother's unblushing ability to tell lies was one of her greatest strengths in her war against Miss Mandeville—that and her inconsistency. Her likes and dislikes, or rather her approvals and disapprovals, were as random as they were rigidly enforced, and picking a way between them was like walking through an uncharted minefield.

Miss Mandeville had read somewhere that laboratory monkeys had been reduced to nervous wrecks by issuing them with conflicting commands and random punishments. It was an effective strategy which, she felt sure, had rid Mother of Papa once she had finished with him. He had been killed during the First World War, struck during an advance by a falling shell which obliterated him so completely that there was nothing left to bury.

Miss Mandeville had only been five when

Papa went off to war, but her memories of him were as vivid as they were few: a small, round, plump man (she had her bony height from her mother's side) with mild, myopic eyes which had often twinkled benignly at Miss Mandeville across the width of the dining table. He was a man of few words, and since he worked hard and long hours, often not returning home from the City until after his daughter was in bed, she had seen little of him. But he was fond of her, and his undemonstrative warmth was a haven from her Mother's cold strictures.

She remembered once sitting on his lap while he told her a story. He had a little, bristly moustache which wagged up and down with the words, and she had watched it, fascinated, as if it were the moustache which was telling the story. He smelled of bay rum and tooth-powder, and his hands were clean and beautiful, and on the end of his gold watch-chain was a guard in the shape of a curious, ugly little pixie with folded legs and a pointed hat, which he had told her was a good-luck charm. 'But don't tell your mother I said so,' he warned her in a lowered voice. 'She doesn't believe in those things.'

He had joined the yeomanry as soon as war was declared and went away to France, and had been killed in the third year, when Miss Mandeville was eight. She had wept immoderately, and had nightmares for years

213

afterwards about his death, for she had not been able to rid herself of the conviction that he had seen the shell coming, and waited for it—had deliberately let it kill him.

In her dreams she saw him standing there on the devastated lunar landscape of the battlefield, looking up at the sky with a small and horrible smile, while the thing came hurtling down towards him, screaming like a steam-kettle, black as a train, to smash him to nothing, teeth, moustache, hands, gold watch-guard and all.

In her dreams she watched in anguish, impotent to protect him, unable even to call out to save him. Once she dreamed that Mother was standing beside her and said, with a kind of grim satisfaction, 'Much good his lucky charm did him!' And in her dream Miss Mandeville had answered, 'That *was* his luck. He wanted to die.'

Was that true? she had wondered, again and again. She was too young when he went away to have had any knowledge or understanding of his relationship with Mother, but the irrational belief remained that Mother had driven him out, and that he had died gladly, rather than return. The only unkindness he had ever shown Miss Mandeville was in thus leaving her at Mother's mercy and, for all the years since, Mother too had driven her away, while keeping her firmly attached to her side. Drawn and repulsed simultaneously with equal

214

force, Miss Mandeville had prescribed a tight orbit around her like a captured moon.

In the growing-up years, Mother had decided everything: what school she should go to, what clothes she should wear, what books she should read, what girls she should be allowed to consort with. (Not 'be friends with'—there was no possibility of that.) She was not allowed to visit other girls in their houses 'in case of germs, dear'. Occasionally she would be directed to invite certain girls home for tea—never those she liked or wanted to get to know, but 'suitable' girls, who would come only because their mothers insisted.

They would sit there, Miss Mandeville and the suitable girls, rigid with embarrassment, avoiding each other's eyes, while Mother held forth on topics dear to her heart. Unless it was raining, they would be taken by Miss Mandeville for a mandatory walk around the large but dull garden, with its sooty shrubbery and regimented plants. Then they would drink milky tea and eat potted-beef sandwiches and the curiously dry cakes from the Hygienic Bakery on Haven Green, and long for it to be over; until finally they were fetched or it was time to go home.

By the time she was old enough to choose her own friends to some extent, she had grown so introverted and awkward that she was unable to make the correct social responses. Those few girls who did not think her queer, or merely dull, she would never invite home. To expose them to the rigours of her gloomy, chilly home would have been to douse what little spark there was between them, and since she was not allowed to meet them anywhere else, her friendships never flourished.

She was good at her lessons, having nothing to distract her from them, and easily won a scholarship to the local high school which, for a wonder, her mother allowed her to take up. Her exam results at the end of high school were good enough for her to have gone to Oxford, and the headmistress even went so far as to write a letter to Mother recommending that Miss Mandeville be allowed to continue her academic career.

But Mother did one of her right-about-turns. When Miss Mandeville had won the scholarship to high school, Mother had said that it was right for every young woman to improve her mind and get herself as good a career as possible, but when it was a question of university, she said that it was a waste of time educating women, who would simply get married and have children. Careers were for men; all a woman needed was some respectable job with which to occupy herself until Mr Right came along.

So Miss Mandeville had not gone to university. Instead she had done a training course in librarianship, and had taken a job in the central library at Walpole Park; and there, thirty-five years later, she worked still, doing the jobs that the young girls just starting were now too highly qualified to want.

They had not been an unhappy thirty-five years, on the whole. She had liked her job, and not only because it got her away from Mother for six days out of seven. She had always loved reading, the great escape, and there she was, surrounded by books all day long. The work was not exacting, her colleagues were mostly kind to her, and she met members of the public who liked to chat, and sometimes even asked her for help. Had Mother understood in the beginning what working in the library would mean to her, she would not have allowed it. But Miss Mandeville learned caution as she grew up: she never spoke about her job if she could help it, and was careful not to express anything warmer than tolerance towards it.

So life had gone on, walking from Castlebar Hill to Walpole Park in the morning—sitting in the staff room, or in the park on fine days, with her sandwiches and a book during the lunch hour—walking home to Castlebar Hill at night, to spend the evening reading, listening to Mother talk, sewing, playing piquet with Mother, or latterly, listening to the wireless.

Other young women went to dances, played tennis, or went on bicycling trips, but Mother would not have allowed Miss Mandeville to accept an invitation to a mixed and unsupervised party, with its implicit impropriety, so it was just as well that no such invitations were ever issued. Sometimes friends of Mother's came round to play bridge, and Miss Mandeville would hand the bridge rolls and sharpen pencils. On Wednesdays and Saturdays the library closed at one, and Mother met her at the door and they went shopping together: John Sanders, or Bensteads, or for a special treat, taking the Tube to Queensway for a look round Whiteley's. On Sundays they went twice to church—Mother was very punctilious in her devotions, and led all the responses in her firm and penetrating contralto. Occasionally she would invite members of the parish council home to tea, and there would be salmon-and-cucumber sandwiches and proper wrapped cake from David Greig's, and Miss Mandeville would fetch more hot water and 'a clean plate for Mr Arbuthnot, dear'.

Only once did Miss Mandeville have a moment of rebellion, and she almost got away, for she was in love, and love made her strong. That was in the summer of 1939. She met him at the library, of course—where else did she ever have a chance to meet people? He was a lecturer in history at University College: a quiet, shy, rather shabby man, whose pepper-and-salt tweed jacket was shapeless with age. Its pockets were stuffed with books, pencils, sheaves of notes, handkerchiefs, pipes and

218

tobacco pouches, and kitchen-sized boxes of matches because he was always mislaying the small ones.

His hair was thick and rather tufty, brown speckled with grey like his jacket, and his eyes behind his glasses were an unexpected, brilliant blue, only he was too shy often to lift them to meet Miss Mandeville's hesitant gaze. He was ten years her senior, and a lifelong bachelor. He had a little house in Madeley Road, a converted cottage which he had bought with money left him by his father, and he had been coming into the central library several days a week for over a year to research a paper he was writing on the effects of the Industrial Revolution on rural life in the villages around London.

Their friendship was slow to grow, for they were both shy, and neither was looking for love. Mr Cartwright had his mind on other things, and Miss Mandeville having lost her father, knew that love made you vulnerable and was best avoided. But they chatted when he visited the library—at first only of his work, for he would ask her for the books he needed, and she would fetch them for him. He admired her efficiency, and after a while if she was occupied when he arrived, he would wait, saying to other, younger assistants, 'No, no, thank you, I'll wait for Miss Mandeville, if you don't mind. She knows what I want.'

Soon he was 'your Mr Cartwright', and

there was a certain amount of agreeable teasing in the staff room. Gradually she came to look forward to his visits. When he came, they would talk of other things besides his work, his blue eyes would lift more frequently to hers, and his shy smile would light his features and make him look younger than his years.

One day he came in asking for a book from the reserve section. They walked up the stairs together, chatting about the political situation and the chances of a pact with Russia, and he stood watching her admiringly as she sought and found the book he required. Something must have been on his mind, for when she turned to him with the book, she saw him absently going about lighting his pipe.

'Oh no,' she cried, putting out a startled hand to stop him. The books in the reserve section were irreplaceable. Her hand touched his, and they both flinched. He dropped his pipe, and she the book, as they both went down on their haunches to retrieve the articles. Their hands reached the book at the same instant, and they froze to immobility, staring at each other, much too close. Then, with what she afterwards realised must have been colossal courage, he cleared his throat and said, 'May I take you out to lunch?'

She was eternally grateful he had said lunch, for had he wanted to meet her after work she would have had to refuse. He took her to lunch twice the first week, to the little restaurant on Springbridge Road (oh, how she feared Mother would pass and look in at the window!). The next week he took her three times, and she almost forgot to worry in the pleasure of finding how much they had in common.

One evening he asked her to go to a recital at the Lyric with him, and she managed it by telling Mother she would be working late at the library, stocktaking. A Wednesday afternoon walk in Kew Gardens was explained away by a toothache and a visit to the dentist. Then he asked her to come to tea on Sunday afternoon, and she told Mother she had been asked to help out at the Sunday School because one of the regular people was ill.

It was a wonderful afternoon. She loved his dear little house—so small and cosy and as different as possible from The Laurels, a stiff, ecclesiastical sort of Victorian villa, dimmed by stained glass the colour of melted cough-drops. She loved his untidy garden and his interesting tea (anchovy toast for one thing; and eccles cakes—imagine!). She loved his company and conversation. Finally, when they washed up together, she loved him. When it went past time for Sunday School to have ended, she lost all sense of self-preservation, and accepted his invitation to stay to supper as though she were a free agent.

Over supper he asked her to call him

Desmond, and she said he should call her Joan. Afterwards they sat on the sofa together, she accepted a whisky-and-soda, and he began to talk of his loneliness; how he had never really noticed it until he had met her, and how, although they had only been seeing each other for a short while, they had really been acquainted for over a year, and how he felt he knew her very well indeed.

Miss Mandeville listened in breathless wonder to words she had never expected to hear, as he rounded off a perfect evening by suggesting that they become engaged, and get married the following spring, when they had had time to get to know each other thoroughly. The bubble burst. Miss Mandeville was reduced to stammering misery. She had to refuse him, she said. Mr Cartwright was made of sterner stuff, and insisted, gently but persistently, on knowing why. At last it all came out in a great surge, all the years of imprisonment and misery, and the hopelessness of knowing that Mother would never allow her to marry, never.

'But my dear Joan,' said Mr Cartwright, 'she simply cannot stop you. You are over twenty-one. You can do as you please. There is nothing in the world she can do to prevent you.'

'You don't know Mother,' Miss Mandeville said. It took him a long time to convince her even that she ought to mention it. She knew that she would be facing terrible trouble when she went home that night for having lied about Sunday School, and it was that, in the end, which persuaded her. If she was going to be in trouble anyway, she might as well be hung for a sheep as a lamb. Mr Cartwright walked her home, but she would not let him come in. She did not want him to be exposed to the first fury. She would face that alone.

It was terrible, more terrible even than she had expected, but love made her strong, and though shrinking and bowing her head, she rode out the storm. At the end of it, defiantly, she said she would not give him up. Mother's eyes narrowed, regarded her shrewdly, and changed tactics.

'Very well, then, I had better meet him. You may bring him to tea next Wednesday.'

It had seemed, then, to Miss Mandeville, a victory. Love made her blind, as well as bold. In delight, triumph and trembling she brought her lover to tea, and presented him to Mother, a Mother wonderfully translated: smiling, charming, delighted to meet Mr Cartwright, sure they would be great friends. She spoke with a rueful laugh of her 'great grown-up daughter' and of wanting nothing but her happiness.

She quizzed Mr Cartwright regally on his family, work, income and prospects. She even, to Miss Mandeville's amazement, spoke of her daughter's academic achievements, and said

223

with a sigh and a laugh, 'Of course, she could have gone to Oxford, but you know what young women are! They want to be out in the world, not bent over dusty old books.'

At the end of it all, Mr Cartwright brought up the subject of their engagement, and Mother had put up no great resistance. Later, when Miss Mandeville took Mr Cartwright to the door, he said to her, 'Well, what was all the fuss about? She was perfectly charming about it.'

'I don't understand,' Miss Mandeville said, dazzled and humbled. 'I've never known her like this before.'

'You're too timid, Joan,' he said, kissing her cheek. 'You've made a dragon of her in your imagination.'

It was later that evening that Mother began to feel unwell, and in the middle of the night she woke Miss Mandeville from a sound sleep and blissful dreams by calling out to her from her bedroom. Miss Mandeville hurried to the bedside. Mother was clutching her chest and panting, her face grey. 'Call Dr Gordon,' she gasped. 'Hurry! I'm dying!'

Dr Gordon suspected a heart attack. Later, when Mother did not die, he diagnosed a severe heart complaint that might take her off at any moment. 'You must avoid sudden shocks at all costs,' he told Miss Mandeville. 'She must be kept absolutely quiet. Complete rest.'

There was no possibility, Miss Mandeville told Mr Cartwright, of their marrying while Mother was so ill. She had to be taken care of all the time. Perhaps at some time in the future, if Mother were stronger, she might broach the subject with her, but she certainly couldn't mention it now. Any upset like that could kill her.

Mr Cartwright argued with her, but she was adamant. He hinted that he didn't entirely believe in Mother's illness, and they quarrelled. He apologised, and they made it up, continuing to have lunch together, but she could not meet him apart from that, for Mother claimed all her spare time.

Then war was declared, and Mr Cartwright joined up. He didn't have to, he volunteered, just as her father had, and went off to war. Just like her father, he never came back. When his letters stopped coming, Mother began to feel better, and when Miss Mandeville's enquiries of the War Office brought her the news that he was missing-believed-killed, Mother rose from her bed a new woman. She was never completely cured of her heart trouble—a thing like that could never be cured, you had it for life, everyone knew that—but she remained pretty hale and hearty, as long as Miss Mandeville didn't do anything to cross her.

And Miss Mandeville didn't. She had no temptation to. Life was so much easier if you didn't struggle against the tide. Her moment of rebellion was over, and Mr Cartwright was gone, and as the years passed she found it difficult to remember what he had looked like.

The war ended and things gradually got back to normal. Then there were reorganisations and innovations, and a new kind of world was born. Suddenly young people were important—the New Elizabethans they called them—and unquestioning obedience to one's elders was no longer the inescapable rule. It was a world of hope and regeneration; of television, atomic power and jet aeroplanes; of beatniks and rock and roll.

Miss Mandeville's life didn't change much. She went on working at the library, issuing books and shelving books, taking enquiries and cataloguing, eating her sandwich lunches and reading novels, and seeing the new employees growing younger year by year as she grew greyer. She knew she was a figure of pity, even of fun to some of them, she knew, but she had her regular customers who came to her rather than the other girls for help and advice, and she knew she was valued.

She thought about Mr Cartwright a lot, and the implications of his having been posted missing. In a novel, she thought, he would come back one day, come walking in through the main door and up to her desk to claim her, and they would go off together hand in hand, into the sunshine and eternal happiness. Of course, that sort of thing didn't happen in real

226

life, and if she looked up every time the door opened, it was not because she thought or even hoped it would be him. She was just interested, that was all.

She didn't think she would really like him to come back, not now, twenty years later. Anticipation was much more satisfying than realisation. Reality was always a disappointment, and Mr Cartwright would probably seem very ordinary and dull to her if she were to meet him now for the first time. Her habitual glance into the shop window daily assured her, he probably would not even recognise her. No, she was better off as she was, with the memory of love, which could never lead to disillusionment or pain.

The great thing was not to regret anything. She didn't regret having loved Mr Cartwright, because that had been wonderful, and she didn't regret having stayed with Mother, because that had been the right thing to do when Mother was so ill. And she didn't regret that evening in 1944 when waves of bombers were coming over and the ack-ack guns on Wormwood Scrubs were making so much noise you could hear them right here in quiet Ealing, and Mother had got herself into a state and said certain things to Miss Mandeville, and Miss Mandeville had given her a treble dose of her heart medicine, which she always mixed with a little medicinal brandy to take away the taste.

Dr Gordon hadn't been at all surprised to be called out, and had comforted Miss Mandeville that these heart patients could pop off at any time, and that it was a blessed release in some ways. He had been very kind to Miss Mandeville. He had called several times after the funeral, to see how she was getting on, and talked a lot about how lonely he was since his wife had died back in 1938. Miss Mandeville had thought that perhaps he was thinking he might ask her to marry him. She had discouraged his calls, and after a while he gave up, retired and sold his practice to a young man, and moved to a bungalow in Hove.

What with The Laurels and insurance and various other matters, Mother had actually left Miss Mandeville rather well off, but she had not been tempted to give up her job at the library. What would she do with herself all day, if she didn't have her work? Go on a cruise? That wasn't her sort of thing at all. She smiled at her reflection and moved on, and joined the crowd waiting at the pedestrian lights to cross over the New Broadway to John Sanders' corner. She must have still been smiling, for as she crossed the road, a man of about her own age crossing from the other direction looked at her curiously, and began to smile as his hand lifted automatically to his hat. She turned her lips down ruefully and shook her head slightly and hurried on. When she got across she stopped in front of the big window of John

Sanders, which was quite an effective mirror, to see if he would look back. But he was already gone, merged into the crowd heading for the station.

She lingered before the shop window to look at the hats, resuming out of habit her inner monologue. Yes, the dull life suited her, for she was really a dull person, as those young things at the library knew very well and made plain when they sniggered about her in the ladies' lavatory, and whispered about all the things they thought she was missing. But the dull life was safe, at all events; and it was good, she thought, to be safe from ever wanting anything, ever again.

HELPING HANDS

HELPING HANDS

The house that Paul and Maggie bought in West Ewell was one of those half-stuccoed nineteen-thirties houses with bay windows, a gable with imitation black-and-white beams, and a stained-glass panel in the front door. Paul, in his lazily amused way, called it 'Arterial Road Tudor', as much in affection as contempt. Maggie called it a Bayko house, because when she was a child, she had had a Bayko Building Set, a device of metal rods and plastic bricks with which you could make up model houses from the pattern book provided. As the Bayko Company was conceived in the thirties and disappeared in the fifties, all the houses in the pattern book had that unmistakable ribbon-development hallmark.

The house was in sound condition, though badly in need of redecoration. The previous owners had lived there for thirty years, and evidently liked the way it had looked when they moved in. They also had a predilection for mauve paintwork and strongly-patterned wallpapers. There were lots of ill-fitting, built-in cupboards, made of chipboard faced with that real wood veneer which had been cunningly processed to look like plastic. When Paul and Maggie first went to look at the house, the owner's wife had pointed them out and proclaimed proudly but quite unnecessarily, 'My husband made all these himself.'

Everybody was saying that the housing market was going up again, so it made sense to buy up to their limit. In fact, the house was probably a bit beyond their limit, but Maggie had loved it so, she had persuaded Paul to go for it. She had never lived in a house before, and having had a somewhat dysfunctional upbringing in a council flat, a semi with a garden front and back represented the apogee of all her childhood dreams, the cosy, middle-class lifestyle her own parents had never attained. She loved it to death, and saw herself in thirty years' time being visited here by her married children, bringing the grandchildren to Sunday lunch.

Paul was not unwilling to be persuaded. The house, because of its naff decorations, did not 'present well' as the estate agents put it, and was therefore probably a little undervalued. These thirties houses were solidly built, and the kitsch of their mock-tudor style was about to make a comeback. All of these things made it a good investment. In five years they would probably clear a very decent profit on it; meanwhile, it was not inconveniently placed for his job.

So they bought it, and when they moved in, they were absolutely wiped out financially. It would take them years to redecorate all the rooms, even if they did most of it themselves. But Maggie was happy. After three and a half years in a bedsitter, sharing a kitchen with two others and a bathroom with five, it was paradise to be in her own house, even if things like the orange nylon carpet would take some living with.

The bathroom was the worst of all. The original black and white tiles and deep cast-iron bath had survived, thank God, but the rest of the room was a symphony of offence. The previous owners had put in a new hand basin and low-level WC in the most repellent shade of turquoise known to man. The wallpaper bore a deafening pattern of blue cabbage-roses and red carnations against a background of ivy-covered trellis, while the ceiling had been covered with polystyrene tiles textured with a honeycomb effect that made Maggie want to scratch. To complete the effect, the woodwork was painted mauve, and the carpet was cherry-red—a colour for which Maggie had never been able to see the justification—with a swirly pattern of black, white and turquoise.

'I suppose,' Maggie said unkindly, 'they thought it was chic to pick out that turquoise motif and feature it in the sanitary ware.'

'It's exactly the sort of thing home decor magazines tell you to do,' Paul said. 'But we can live with it for now. In a week or two, we probably won't even notice it.'

Maggie stared at him. 'You jest.'

'Well, we can't do everything,' he said reasonably. 'It's much more important to get the sitting room and main bedroom done.'

Maggie did not agree. 'Some things are beyond endurance, and this bathroom's one of them.'

Maggie saw with alarm that a frown was gathering between Paul's brows. It was a thing that had happened more often since they first started looking for a house. Everyone said that buying a house was a stressful experience, but she had assumed that they were different: too balanced, and too much in love to take it out on each other.

But looking for houses had certainly pointed up some basic differences of approach between them. Paul looked on a house as an investment in bricks and mortar, while to Maggie it was first and foremost a home. The worry was that disagreement often produced that frown from Paul, coupled with a withdrawal from the argument, as though it was self-evident that he was right and there was no more to be said. Naturally, this infuriated Maggie. She had always thought there was nothing more irritating than to be agreed with for the sake of peace, but to have your arguments regarded as irrelevant was infinitely more galling.

This, she remembered with foreboding, was what Paul's mother had done to her from the very first meeting. It was a formidable weapon

236

for getting your own way, and Mrs Manley had already had her own way in a number of things. It was by her will, for instance, that they had got married at all. They had wanted simply to live together. Maggie was firmly against the institution of marriage, and Paul was indifferent to the whole issue.

'When are you two going to get married?' Mrs Manley had asked. 'You'll have to do it before you start looking for a house, or there'll be trouble over the mortgage.'

'Oh no, they don't mind about that nowadays,' Maggie explained kindly. 'It's simply based on the income of the individuals.'

Mrs Manley's eyes grew flinty with denial, but she merely changed her ground. 'Nevertheless, you'll have to think about marriage soon. It isn't fair on the children to let them in for that sort of gossip. Not everybody has liberal ideas.' From the tone of her voice, liberal was evidently a perjorative term.

'We haven't even talked about starting a family,' Maggie said, half amused, half annoyed by the speed of Mrs Manley's assumptions. 'I'm not sure I shall want children.'

Mrs Manley's brows contracted to a frown. 'Paul will want a family,' she said firmly, as if that was all there was to be said about that, and left the room.

Some days later, addressing herself to Paul

over the Sunday lunch table, she said, 'I was thinking, dear, about the first Saturday in July for the wedding, before people start going away. I've spoken to Mr Twemlow, and that fits in nicely with holidays, because he goes the last week of July and the first week of August, and Mr Butts has the middle two weeks.'

'Who's Mr Butts?' Paul asked vaguely.

'You remember, dear, the organist. A June wedding would be nice, only they'll still be repairing the tower, and you don't want scaffolding in your photographs, do you? But Mr Twemlow says they've promised to be finished by the end of June.'

Maggie was about to protest at this organisation of her life when Paul caught her eye and shook his head firmly, enjoining her to silence. Against her will, she subsided until Mrs Manley went out to fetch the pudding.

'Why d'you let her go on like that?' she burst out in an agonised whisper. 'Before you know where you are, she'll have us marching up the aisle with bridesmaids, Mendelssohn and the lot!'

'Oh well, it won't kill us.' Paul said. 'If we mean to live together, what does it matter whether we're married or not? And it'll please Mother no end.'

Maggie stared at him with astonishment. The tone of his voice suggested it was already a settled thing. 'Wait a minute, have you been discussing it with her behind my back?'

'Don't be silly,' he said—which wasn't saying yes and it wasn't saying no. 'She's always looked forward to my wedding, ever since I was a kid, and she's getting on in years. We shouldn't really put it off, or it might be too late. It won't hurt us to please her in this one little thing, will it?'

'It's not a little thing to me,' Maggie said indignantly, but Paul hushed her.

'Not now. She's coming back. We'll talk about it tonight.'

Talk revealed only that Paul had already materially submitted to his mother's demands. He reasoned that since they didn't care about being married and Mother did, they ought to go along with her. Weddings were never really for the couple, anyway, but for the family. Mother had been planning it in her mind ever since she had first met Maggie, and it would break her heart not to be allowed to see it through.

Maggie gave in, though feeling half ashamed of herself for abandoning her principles, on the grounds that it was the generous and compassionate thing to do. So they got married, in Mrs Manley's local church, where Paul had been christened and Mr Manley buried, with morning suits, white dress, bridesmaids, a reception and speeches; all the things Maggie had long despised. Mrs Manley organised everything.

'After all dear, it's usually the father of the

bride's privilege to play host, but you are a wee bit short of family, aren't you?'

And to do Paul justice, Maggie acknowledged that had her mother been alive, she would have been just as eager for a church wedding as his mother.

But that had been only the beginning. 'Don't think I'm going to be forever interfering,' Mrs Manley said with a gay smile. 'The last thing newly-weds want is in-laws hanging around giving them good advice. You won't find me forever appearing on your doorstep.'

Thereafter she appeared on the doorstep several times a week, and on the days when she didn't visit, she held long conversations with Paul on the telephone. On Sundays they were expected to go to lunch at Mrs Manley's house, 'Because,' she would say with that irritating little laugh, 'I know you young wives don't like cooking, and Paul does so love his roast beef and Yorkshire.'

It was not until they bought the house that Mrs Manley revealed herself fully. From the moment they moved in, she haunted the place, offering advice, choosing colour-schemes, pointing out defects. When Paul gave her a spare key, Maggie's temper boiled over.

'I can't move now without tripping over her, but if she has her own key, she'll be letting herself in while I'm out and snooping through my things!'

240

Paul grew chilly with offence. 'My mother does not snoop.'

'She bloody well does!' Maggie said trying, not entirely successfully, to make it sound jokey. 'What about last Saturday? She went upstairs to the bathroom, and when I went up a bit later she was in our room looking through the chest of drawers.'

'She wasn't snooping,' Paul said, ultra-reasonable. 'She was just checking whether we had enough towels, because she wanted to buy us some more. She told you so herself.'

'Oh sure, that's what she said. And in any case, I don't want her buying us towels. That sort of thing is just the thin end of the wedge. She only does it to make us feel grateful.'

'Oh come on, darling,' Paul said, frowning. 'You make her sound like some sort of Machiavelli. She's just an ordinary widow, a bit lonely, wanting to do something nice for her only son. What's so wrong with that? Don't be so mean. She hasn't had much happiness since Dad died.'

Maggie couldn't argue any further without putting herself in the wrong, since Paul evidently believed Mrs Manley's own view of herself, he would only get more angry with her for insisting that his mother had him exactly where she wanted him.

She changed ground. 'I just don't want her to keep doing things around the house. I want to have the fun of choosing things for myself.

241

Can't you understand that?'

Feeling he had won, Paul was prepared to be generous. He put an arm round her. 'Of course, darling. I'll have a word with her. And I'm sorry about the key, but she asked me straight out, and I couldn't think of a way to say no without hurting her feelings. But I'm sure she won't use it unless she's invited.'

Maggie was sure she would—and Maggie was right. Mrs Manley was rapidly proving herself a very large fly in the ointment.

It wasn't just the criticisms, always delivered with such sweet reasonableness. 'I don't think you ought to leave meat unwrapped in the fridge, dear. It isn't hygienic. They don't do it in restaurants, you know, or they'd be prosecuted'. 'Do you find that ready-made pastry quite satisfactory? I don't think it can ever be as good as one's own—but then,' with that little laugh, 'Paul always loved my pastry so. He used to say no-one else could make it like me'.

It wasn't even just coming home to find jobs done for her, furniture moved, and things put away so that she couldn't find them. 'I moved that table over to the other side of the room, dear. I expect you didn't realise, but sunlight will take all the colour out of the wood'. 'I did that little bit of washing up you left. I expect you had to dash off to work in a hurry, but I don't think it's nice leaving dirty dishes about all day'.

No, most of all, it was the 'little presents' which kept appearing, requiring every time a gratitude Maggie didn't feel and resented having to simulate. She was being swamped, smothered, and taken over. Her house was no longer her own. It wouldn't have been so bad if the presents had been articles either of use or beauty, but Mrs Manley's taste ran a steady course between the hideous and the useless. She seemed determined that Paul's house should resemble as closely as possible his childhood home, hazardous with knick-knacks and gadgets.

'What do we want a musical cigarette box for?' she raved at Paul one evening, at the end of her tether. 'Neither of us smokes.'

'Why are you always so ungrateful?' Paul countered with a frown. 'Mother means well. I expect she thought it was pretty.'

'Pretty? Look at it! Views of the Alps, painted by a rather untalented two-year-old, no doubt to complement the fact that when you open the lid, it plays the theme from *The Sound of Music*. How witty!'

'Well, you can keep buttons in it or something, can't you? Mother likes buying us little things.'

'We haven't even got a sideboard to put it on,' Maggie said with bitter irony. 'If we did, it could stand next to the slop-bowl with the yellow roses on it that she gave us last week.'

Now Paul lost his temper. 'Look, I'm just

about sick of you making snide remarks about my mother. She does her very best to be nice to you, but nothing she ever does is right, is it?'

'She could try minding her own business, only she'd find that a bit too difficult, wouldn't she?'

'How can you talk like that after all she's done for us? You ought to be grateful to her.'

'I don't want to be grateful to her! I don't want her to spend money on us! I don't want her horrible presents! I don't like them, I never asked for them!'

'How can you be so mean-minded? She's lonely and she wants to feel she's important to us.'

'I'm sorry she's lonely, but that's not my fault. I've got my own life to lead and I wish she'd just leave us alone!'

Paul gave her a cold look, and rose from his chair. 'I think I'll go upstairs and read. You seem to be getting hysterical.' He withdrew with icy dignity, and when he had gone, Maggie gave vent to a short scream and threw a cushion at the door.

Perhaps the quarrel had not been entirely destructive. For the next couple of weeks, Mrs Manley's visits were much less frequent, and Maggie thought that Paul must have spoken to her and asked her to ease off. She felt a genuine gratitude, tried her best to be friendly to the old lady when she did appear, and made her peace with Paul by being extra nice to him

244

in bed and telling him that his mother certainly could make a delicious Dundee cake.

It was during this ceasefire period that Maggie was given a rise at work, which, being backdated, resulted in an unexpected lump sum. She proposed at once to use it to have the bathroom redecorated. Paul was doubtful, but she remembered the upsets of the past few weeks, and instead of flaring up and telling him she'd do what she liked with her own money, she restrained herself and tried coaxing him.

'Oh please, Paul, do consider it. I know we were going to do all our own decorating and save money, but a bathroom's difficult, with all the odd corners and pipes and things. It really needs a professional job.'

'But there are so many other things that need doing first. The bathroom can wait.'

'Yes, I know, but I do so love to bath in comfort, and I just hate that paper and that awful mauve paint. We both work so hard, we ought to have some luxury in life. Do say yes, Paul, please.'

'Oh look, it's your money, you can do what you like with it,' he said, not entirely disagreeably. 'I hope I'll have some say in the colour-scheme?'

'Of course,' she said. 'Though with that awful turquoise suite, we won't have a completely free hand. I'd really like to have it ripped out and replaced, but my pay-rise won't stretch to that.'

'Replaced with what?'

'Well, I thought it would be terrific to do the whole thing in thirties style, to go with the house. All in black and white, with perhaps an art deco mirror over the basin, a high-level cistern and a wooden toilet-seat.'

Paul liked the idea, and they discussed it pleasantly, more like their old selves than they had been for a long time. At last he said, 'You know, it would be a pity to spoil the ship for a ha'porth of tar. Let's find out what it would cost to do the whole room just as we want it.'

'It would cost more than my lump sum,' Maggie said.

'I'm not entirely penniless. Let's get an estimate, and if it isn't too much more, I'm sure we can manage to scrape the money together somehow. You deserve your bit of luxury, my love.'

'Oh Paul!' Maggie remembered why she had married him, and flung herself into his arms in a delight that ended up, most satisfactorily, in bed.

It must have been about that time that she conceived, for a fortnight later, when the estimate for the work came in from the decorators, she missed her first period, and by the time the job was completed, she was sure.

Either being pregnant had changed her nature, or Mrs Manley had modified her behaviour, for during those weeks of the

246

rebuilding, she didn't seem to get on Maggie's nerves at all. She was naturally very excited when told about the baby, but Maggie found her pleasure rather touching. Also it was suddenly rather scary to become responsible for a new life, and not having a mother of her own to turn to, Maggie was glad to have someone on hand who had been through it before. Mrs Manley's advice was surprisingly sensible and reassuring.

'Don't let Paul fuss you, and don't read any of those books. They'll only worry you for no reason. Having a baby is completely natural, it's what we're made for, so you just relax and enjoy it. And anything you want me to do, just ask. Oh I'm so excited, I can't tell you! I'm going to start buying baby things as soon as the shops open tomorrow.' And even that didn't seem the threat it would have been a few weeks ago.

The bathroom job seemed to be charmed: it went through without a hitch, and in record time. The end result was even better than Maggie had envisaged. They managed to find a carpet whose large irregular trapezoids of black and white matched the room not only in colour but in thirties feeling, and a reproduction art deco mirror. Paul bought a dear little wicker stool which he painted white, and Maggie treated herself to a Lalique glass vase for the windowsill.

It was worth every penny, Maggie assured

Paul on the day the last of the workmen left. It had cost, first and last, about twice the sum Maggie had in hand, but Paul had paid up without blinking. Each of them had a personal bank account, out of which they paid for lunches, fares, clothes and so on, as well as the joint account for household expenses. After the Lalique vase, Maggie's was teetering on the verge of red, and she assumed that Paul's was too, and was touched that he had allowed her this—face it, he was right—unnecessary extravagance of the luxury bathroom.

'Oh, but I love it!' she cried. 'I'm going to spend all my spare time in the bath from now on!'

Mrs Manley was also impressed when she came to visit and Maggie, still suffering under the effects of good humour, took her upstairs to look at it.

'It's very nice, dear, very smart indeed,' Mrs Manley said. 'It quite takes me back. We used to see a lot of this modern style when I was a girl. Futuristic, I'd call it.' She looked around with a satisfied smile. 'They've certainly done a nice job. It pays to have good workmen, you know, and I must say I don't begrudge a penny. I had my doubts when Paul first asked me, because there are so many other things that need doing around the house. But as long as you're pleased—and now I see it, I don't think it was money wasted.'

She turned back to her daughter-in-law,

without seeming to see the dull rage which was suffusing her face. 'And I've got a little present for you,' she went on. 'I noticed you hadn't got one. Actually, when I saw this one, I couldn't resist it, because it was just so right. Here you are, dear, with my best wishes.'

She presented to Maggie a flat, lumpy package wrapped in tissue paper, which Maggie, still wordless with astonishment and fury, took from her automatically and opened. Inside was a knitted thing, like a badly made stuffed toy: a lady in a crinoline dress. The skirt part was not stuffed, but simply an empty woollen bell-shape. The doll's face had a simpering smile stitched onto it, and the arms stood out stiffly to either side like a gesture of surrender. Maggie stared at it speechlessly, unable to understand what it was she had been given.

'Isn't it sweet?' Mrs Manley exclaimed. 'I saw it at the church jumble sale last week. Mrs Twemlow knitted it herself. You know, the dear vicar's wife. She has one just like it in her bathroom, only in blue. It was such a coincidence that she did this one in black and white. She knits them up out of odd balls that people give her for charity, and when I saw this one—well, it seemed sort of meant, you know.'

'What is it?' Maggie managed to ask faintly. Mrs Manley looked astonished.

'Don't you really know? Goodness!' She snatched it from Maggie's nerveless fingers and darted over to where the spare toilet roll sat on the new wicker stool beside the pedestal, and dropped the doll over it, twitching it into place so that the toilet roll was concealed under the skirt and the doll sat coyly on top, arms outstretched, smiling as though butter wouldn't melt in her mouth. 'There, you see? All neatly hidden. So much nicer, don't you think? Because I didn't like to say so before, dear, but it really isn't very nice just to leave it out like that for everyone to see.'

Maggie didn't know whether to laugh or cry, and what actually came out was a sort of hoarse sob.

*   *   *

That night she could hardly wait for Mrs Manley to go home before initiating the worst row of their lives together, married or unmarried.

'How could you do a thing like that to me?' she cried again and again, and Paul shrugged his shoulders and looked astonished.

'What on earth's got into you? You wanted your bathroom, didn't you? And now you've got it. Mother was pleased to help. I don't know what you're making a fuss about.'

'Don't you? Then why didn't you tell me it was your mother's money?'

He scowled. 'Because you're always so unreasonable about Mother. For God's sake, what does it matter who paid for it? Are you going to be like this all through pregnancy? Because if you are—'

'It's nothing to do with being pregnant!' she shrieked. 'Can't you see? It's like asking her permission to have things done. I don't want her deciding everything in our married life! I don't want her decorating my house! The next thing she'll be choosing my clothes and deciding what books I read.'

'Oh don't be so silly! You're being totally unreasonable.'

'I don't know why you bothered to marry me. You should have stayed home with her. It would have saved you the trouble of trying to make this house into a replica of hers.'

'All she wants to do is give us a helping hand to start up our own home. What's so wrong with that?'

'That's not what she wants! She wants to take over. She never wanted to give you up, and this is her way of making sure she doesn't have to. She's smothering me out of existence, so it can be just you and her again.'

'You're just being totally hysterical. My mother's a perfectly ordinary, kind, nice person, and any normal woman could get on with her without all this fuss. But you're so ungrateful—'

'Ungrateful!' Maggie glared at him for one murderous moment, and then flung out of the room. 'I'm going to bed—alone!'

'Good thing too!' Paul shouted after her, and she ran upstairs to the spare room and flung herself down on the bed, sobbing.

*   *   *

Eventually nature asserted itself and she fell asleep, waking in the middle of the night to find herself stiff and cramped from her unnatural position face-down on the bed. Paul must have come in and pulled the counterpane over her, and she thrust it back and sat up wearily. The counterpane was pink candlewick, a gift from Paul's mother for the spare-room bed which she no doubt hoped would be designated her own. Maggie had always hated candlewick. Where in the house could she go to escape from Mrs Manley's presence? The woman was everywhere—it was like eyes, watching her. Even her dream bathroom would now always be haunted.

Thinking of the bathroom reminded her that she needed to go to the loo—one of the hazards of pregnancy. She got up off the bed and went cautiously to the door. The house was in darkness, and there was no sound, so presumably Paul had gone to bed. She didn't switch on any lights, not wanting to wake him, but padded through the familiar darkness to the bathroom, and eased the door closed behind her.

It smelled of fresh paint and new carpet,

and a great sadness came over her as she sat down on the mahogany seat and hunched forward, leaning her elbows on her knees. She had wanted this bathroom so, and loved it so, and now it was spoiled. It was not hers, it was Paul's mother's, granted out of her power and paid for with her money, ruled over by her totem, the ghastly little knitted idol of the spare toilet roll, her mark, her representative. Maggie had wanted this one room to reflect her taste, and hers alone; one last little gesture of independence before she was subsumed into Mrs Manley's obliterating all-presence. Paul's mother was like one of those primitive goddesses that demanded endless propitiation and blood-sacrifices.

Head in hands, Maggie paused a moment and wondered if she were being unreasonable. Wasn't this just normal in-law difficulties, the sort of adjusting and settling down every relationship had to go through? Marriage was something you had to work at, you couldn't just dump it because it turned out not to be absolutely straightforward. Besides, now she was pregnant, she had a sort of hostage to fortune, she couldn't just cut her losses and walk out. And then she thought of the baby, and depression settled over her again. She was trapped. It wouldn't be her baby, it would be theirs. Mrs Manley would take it over, ever-so-kindly, and Paul would tell her to be grateful that his mother did so much to help her while he fed her baby to the wolf-goddess.

Oh God, she thought, I'm in a mess, and what do I do to sort it out? If only she had someone to turn to, someone who would give her impartial advice, someone with an outside perspective. This was a crisis point in her life, and she really, really needed a helping hand, but the only advice available was from the source of the problem. She felt so smothered and overwhelmed and confused, she really didn't know if she were being unreasonable or not. Surely it was unreasonable to feel Mrs Manley was taking her over? She was just, as Paul said, an ordinary widow—surely Maggie could cope with that? It wasn't as if she had supernatural powers.

She shivered; she must go back to bed. She couldn't sit here on the loo all night. She reached for the loo-roll, and found that the one on the holder was finished, and whoever had used it up had not changed it. Typical! Even in the minutiae, life was against her. Automatically she put out her hand for the spare roll on the wicker stool beside her, and it was at that moment that, out of the darkness, two little knitted hands took hold of hers and patted it kindly.

CULTURE VULTURE

CULTURE VULTURE

The late afternoon sun shone on the Sussex hills, on the little village of Glynde, and on the pleasant red-brick house of Glyndebourne. The sunshine lay as fat as butter over well-manicured lawns, herbaceous beds planted out in a co-ordinated scheme of blue and white, the broad meadows beyond the ha-ha where placid cattle grazed. It dappled the tree-fringed lake, flinging nets of diamonds about the water-lilies; it defined slices of inviting shadow along the edges of the croquet lawn and the sunken garden; and it glittered fiercely off the chrome and glass of a hundred cars parked nose-downwards in ranks across the hillside car park. For Glyndebourne was suffering its annual invasion: at this very moment the Glyndebourne Opera Company was performing *Simon Boccanegra* to a polite and evening-dress-clad audience—some of whom had never been to an opera before and, longing for the dinner interval as for deliverance from durance vile, were damned sure they weren't coming back in for the second half.

They were lucky with the weather this year, anyway, thought Detective Inspector Bill Slider, mooching about the grounds. Since the beginning of the season, the weather had been splendid. There had been two wet days earlier this week, but yesterday the wind had gone round again, and now it looked set fair for another long spell.

The gardens were infested with portable tables, folding chairs and tartan car rugs, empty champagne bottles, plastic wine coolers, tupperware bowls full of lettuce, Marks and Spencer biscuits-for-cheese, Sainbury's after dinner mints, containers of every sort ranging from wicker hampers to plastic carrier bags. All the paraphernalia of middle-class picnics blossomed like *lusus naturae* in the favoured corners where people had rushed in early to stake their claims in advance of the long interval. Slider pondered to himself the mystery of why people so keen on eating *al fresco* always huddled together round the edges of the lawns, never setting up in the middle of one where there was plenty of room. If they were so afraid of the wide open spaces, why didn't they just stay indoors?

He was only here because Joanna was playing in the pit, and it was a pleasant way to spend his day off. They had had their picnic for their lunch on the way down; in the interval the orchestra always decamped to the Trevor Arms in the village, for a pint of Harvey's and a plate of egg and chips. 'Anything to get away from the punters,' said Joanna's dour desk-partner, rolling his eyes. 'If they spot you, the buggers come up and want to talk about *music*!' So much for culture.

An electric bell sounded from the direction of the house, warning him that the first half was over. Slider turned and walked back towards it. Inside, the audience would be applauding, the cast bowing, and the orchestra stampeding out as fast as their legs and the restricted headroom would allow—it wasn't called the pit for nothing. Since he had been involved with Joanna, Slider had learned a great deal about the world of music, and he had discovered that the most essential skill an orchestral musician could have was the ability to pack up fast and get out before the punters. Joanna could stow her fiddle so fast it would make your head spin—which was why it was surprising and even annoying when she did not immediately appear. Slider waited, expecting every moment to see her come dashing out of the side door holding her long black dress clear of her ankles; but here was the audience, pouring out, clogging the paths and lawns. Rapid movement would be out of the question now. Precious interval time would be wasted.

Then he saw her, beckoning from the scenery door. She was with someone. Slider headed towards them. The man she was with was tall, young and handsome—the bastard—with aristocratic features and a confident air. Everything about him was impeccable—his dinner-suit, his patent leather shoes, his glossy hair, his gleaming teeth—even his skin seemed to have that extra lustre that can only come from generations of selective breeding. Joanna was listening to him, smiling and nodding, but she glanced towards Slider with something of anxiety or apology in her expression.

'Oh, Bill, this is Justin Phillips. He's the Establishments Director here.' She completed the introduction. 'Detective Inspector Bill Slider.'

Phillips smiled an impeccable smile and offered his beautifully manicured hand. Slider restrained himself from wiping his own down the back of his trousers before grasping it. It was no good: this marvellous, impervious confidence of the moneyed and public-school educated always made him feel grubby.

'Inspector Slider,' Phillips said, 'Or may I call you Bill?'

Do I have a choice? Slider thought, but aloud he only said, 'How do you do.'

'I'm so sorry to break into your free time like this, but Joanna thought you might just be willing to help us. We have a little problem, you see, and hearing that you were in the CID—well, I thought it was worth asking, at least.'

'What's the problem?' Slider asked.

'I'm afraid we've got a petty thief,' Phillips said.

The luscious pint and the egg and chips receded before Slider's eyes like a ghost at cock-crow. He supposed things like this

260

happened to doctors all the time, people coming up to them at parties, describing their symptoms and asking advice. 'I've got this awful rash, you see—it goes all the way from here to here—'

'How petty?' Slider asked.

'Well, at first it was nothing really valuable; small change, costume jewellery, odds and ends. It was annoying more than anything, though there was quite a spate of it. Then for two days it stopped, and we all gave a sigh of relief, thinking it was over. But last night it escalated beyond petty theft. Our diva lost a pair of diamond earrings, and I'm afraid they were real diamonds.'

'When did she miss them? Are you sure she hasn't just mislaid them?'

'*She* seems to be sure,' Phillips said. 'She put them on the table in her dressing room while she took a shower. When she came out, they were gone.'

'And when did these thefts begin?'

'Two weeks ago. The first loss was reported on the day of the first performance.'

'So you think it's a member of the company, do you?'

Joanna said, 'The company was all here for three weeks before that, rehearsing. There was no trouble until the audiences arrived.'

'And the things seem to go missing just before or during the performance,' Phillips added.

261

'But the audience would be inside the theatre during the performance, wouldn't they?' Slider asked.

'There's nothing to stop someone *not* going in, except the price of the tickets,' Phillips said with a glimmer of humour. 'Of course, on the other hand, there's nothing to stop anyone coming into the grounds. A place like this is impossible to police: backstage is like a rabbit warren, the house is large and rambling, there are dozens of entrances and exits. And with all the people wandering round—singers, musicians, stage hands, caterers—to say nothing of their friends . . . Well, anyone could walk about the corridors and never be asked what they were doing there.'

Slider looked at Joanna, who shrugged and made a complicated face which said, 'I know, I'm sorry, but he insisted, what could I do?'

'Well, I'm not sure that I'll be able to do anything,' Slider said, as kindly as he could. 'You've reported the theft to the local police, I suppose?'

Phillips looked embarrassed. 'Well no, actually, not yet. You see, we hoped we might be able to clear it up without that. Our insurance company is going to be very unhappy about it, and the premiums will go through the roof, and besides that, to complicate matters, we did actually find one of the earrings.'

'Where?'

'In the grounds, down by the bottom lake. I suppose the thief must have dropped it while making his escape.'

Slider sighed inwardly. 'You really ought to bring the local police in. You should have called them straight away—they might have found some evidence to help them. Now I suppose every man and his dog will have been tramping all over everything.'

Phillips almost hung his head. 'Yes, I suppose you're right. Oh dear. I really didn't want to have to make this official. But will you just have a look yourself, in an informal way? As a favour. Since you're here. Maybe your trained eye will spot something.'

'I'll have a quick look,' Slider said. It wouldn't make any difference now, and Joanna was looking at him appealingly. 'But you must make an official approach to the police, or you won't be able to claim on the insurance.'

'Yes, I understand. Where would you like to go first?'

'The dressing room,' Slider said.

It was on the first floor; a small room with a bed, a wardrobe, a sofa, and a table under the window. Through a second door was a small bathroom with wc, basin and shower cubicle. The room was untidy with clothes, toiletries, newspapers and discarded tissues, and the air was heavy with the smell of face-powder.

'The earrings were on that table,' Phillips

said.

'And was the window open?'

'Yes. But the door wasn't locked. Anyone could have slipped in while she was in the shower. She probably wouldn't hear someone knock on the door while the water was running.'

Who's the detective, you or me? Slider thought. He went over to the window and looked out. The face of the house was thick with creeper, and a blackbird shot out from it with an alarmed *puck* as he leaned out. The sun was glinting on a hundred windows, mostly set open to let in the sweet, warm air.

'The other thefts, where did they take place?' he asked.

'Other dressing rooms on this floor, and one from a bedroom upstairs.'

'Nothing from ground-floor rooms?'

'No,' said Phillips, after a moment's thought. 'But I suppose it's quieter up here— there'd be more people milling about downstairs.'

'A crowd is the best cover,' Slider said. 'If you see one lone person in a corridor, you're more likely to remember what they look like.'

They couldn't have come up the creeper anyway, Slider noted mentally: it wouldn't have taken the weight, and there was no sign of damage. Besides, there'd be no need for a window job, with all the doors open.

'All right,' he said, 'you can show me where

the earring was found. Who found it, by the way?'

'One of the gardeners.'

'Do you trust him?'

'Oh, gosh, yes. He's been with us for years. Besides, if he'd stolen them, why on earth would he hand just one in? As a pair they're worth much more than the value of the stones.'

'You did look for the other one, I suppose?' Slider said.

'Of course,' Phillips said, offended. 'I say, look, when we get downstairs, would you mind if we just sort of strolled about, as though we were taking a walk. I don't want to alarm anyone.'

There were three lakes, of descending size, separated by sluice gates. Trees and bushes flanked them, which in the mild evening light were riotous with birdsong. Blackbirds and robins proclaimed territory from the treetops; a thrush repeated itself maddeningly from a thicket; a pair of magpies, flipping their tails, went off like football rattles; a heavy crash overhead followed by a frantic noise of flapping told of a pair of wood pigeons choosing the flimsiest twig of a silver birch on which to try and matc. On the surface of the lake, a moorhen family was puttering about, and every now and then one of the chicks, finding itself left behind, would hoist itself bodily out of the water and run flatfooted across the floating lily leaves.

'It must be an absolute paradise for birds,' Slider remarked. 'Water, trees, peace and quiet.'

'Yes,' said Phillips. 'We get some quite rare birds from time to time, especially down by the bottom lake, where it's much more overgrown. The audience hardly ever go down there—they usually stick to the circuit of the top lake.'

'Well, that's something,' Slider said. Despite yesterday's rain, the path around the top lake was perfectly dry, and beaten smooth by dozens of feet; even now there were couples strolling around it. At the end was a half-rotten gate, beyond which the vegetation grew more densely along the bank of the second lake. The path there was partly grassed, partly bare earth, and there were a few puddles still to be seen.

'The path doesn't drain as well here,' Phillips said. 'And it gets wilder and damper the further you go.'

'We'd better stick to the grass,' Slider said, 'just in case there's anything to be learned from the soft patches.' Though the days of being able to identify a man from the soles of his shoes had ended with the coming of trainers. Eat your heart out, Lord Peter. 'Where does this path go eventually?'

'Beyond the bottom lake it joins up with the farm track, which leads eventually to the farm yard,' said Phillips.

'So it would be possible for an intruder to enter or leave the premises that way?'

'Oh yes,' said Phillips. 'If they wanted to.'

Exactly, Slider thought, why should they want to, with such free access from the front? Beyond the next gate, the path was barely discernible through the long grass and nettles. It was fringed with bushes and brambles, overhung with trees, dim and green in the westering light, and the air was filled with the peppery smell of damp ditches, water weed, elder and kex. An unseen duck quacked mysteriously from behind the rushes, as though commenting on the folly of mankind.

'This is where the earring was found, just here, under this tree,' Phillips said. 'I got him to show me exactly. In the grass, just here.'

Slider could see that there'd be nothing here for forensic—which at least would mean he wouldn't get into trouble for spoiling the site. Still, just to show willing, he squatted down to examine the spot more closely, and he saw something glint in the grass. He leaned forward. It was the ring-pull from a drinks can. Oh, the thrill of the chase! He was about to stand up again when he saw another a little further off, and another, and then, close to the bowl of the tree, a small silver mustard-spoon. Lager and mustard? What kind of a picnic did that suggest? He stared for a long moment, and then looked up into the branches of the tree above him, an idea forming in his mind.

267

He stood up. 'It was definitely just here that the earring was found?'

'Definitely,' said Phillips.

'Well, if you can get someone to bring a ladder down here, there's a chance we might be able to find the other one.'

* * *

'I didn't know they really did that,' Joanna said when they met again after the second half.

'They do,' Slider said. 'Especially now they're getting so much more used to people, living on top of us. All the corvidae are curious.'

'It seems so obvious. I wonder why Phillips didn't think of it.'

'He's not a genius like me,' said Slider modestly. 'I wondered from the first about the windows because he said there'd been no thefts for two days before yesterday, and those were the days when the weather broke. It was cold and wet, and the windows would have been shut. But when I looked at the creeper, I could see no-one could have climbed up it, and it was hardly likely anyone could have put a ladder up without someone noticing. And besides, if the windows, why not the ground-floor windows?'

'Well, I'm really glad it turned out all right,' she said, rather jerkily because they were hurrying towards the car park. Getting out before the audience was doubly important at the end of the evening. 'Phillips was as pleased as a terrapin with two tails.' A low noise erupted behind them. 'Oh God, here come the punters. We'd better run, or we'll get stuck in the traffic jam, and I can't go without my pint a second time.'

It was when they were standing by the car and she was waiting for him to open it that she said, 'But was that really all that put you onto it—the open windows?'

Slider looked at her. 'What a question, and you a musician! Opera was rather on my mind, given where we are.' And he hummed a few bars of Rossini.

A slow smile spread across her face. 'I'm sorry to spoil your gloat,' she said, 'but that was *La Scala di Seta*, not *La Gazza Ladra*!'

'What?' he said in dismay. 'Curses, another perfectly good theory gone west!' And then he shrugged. 'Oh well, I suppose it comes out the same, in a spiritual sort of way.'

We hope you have enjoyed this Large Print book. Other Chivers Press or Thorndike Press Large Print books are available at your library or directly from the publishers.

For more information about current and forthcoming titles, please call or write, without obligation, to:

Chivers Press Limited
Windsor Bridge Road
Bath BA2 3AX
England
Tel. (01225) 335336

OR

Thorndike Press
P.O. Box 159
Thorndike, Maine 04986
USA
Tel. (800) 223-2336

All our Large Print titles are designed for easy reading, and all our books are made to last.